Hope and Desire

Theresa Grant

PublishAmerica
Baltimore

ISBN: 1-4137-5860-6
PUBLISHED BY PUBLISHAMERICA, LLLP
www.publishamerica.com
Baltimore

Printed in the United States of America

Dedication

This book is dedicated to my family: Dr. Warren H. Grant, Jennifer Caron, Warren H. 3rd and Kevin A. Grant.

Acknowledgments

I want to thank my teachers: Suzanne James of UniversalClass.Com, and Evelyn B. Kelly of Long Ridge Writers School for their help and inspiration.

Dear Claudette,

The theme of this book is believe in yourself. No matter what others may say or think, persue your dreams with a passion, and keep hope alive. Without hope there is no life.

Desire fuels our soul and fires our passion, but be careful of what you desire. It may not be what you wanted.

Love,
Theresa Grant

Prologue

Rap music reverberated through the kitchen's ceiling like a sonic boom. Jennifer sprang from the dilapidated kitchen chair, and a blast of heat from the opened screened door greeted her. She stared at herself in the wall mirror behind the kitchen table, as sweat trickled down her smooth milk chocolate face, staining her meticulously applied, honey-amber, Fashion Fair Foundation. She sat back at the table, and turned the small fan with the rusty blades toward her face. "Bill," she yelled, and gave her head a vehement shake. Her long dark auburn hair slid around her delicate round shoulders.

"Darn his hide!" She retrieved the broom from the pantry, and banged the ceiling with the handle. "Cut the noise, Bill." She banged again, harder. "Lower the volume."

A stupid boy. What a headache! Nutcase...acting like a ghetto punk. Leave the loud sound outside. Why can't I live in a nicer neighborhood? New Jersey Avenue stinks with dope peddlers, roustabouts, and homeless men lurking to cop a buck.

The smoke detector, above the door, blared and added irritation to her already frayed nerves.

"Darn, the gravy boiled over!" Smoke hit her full in the eyes and penetrated her nostrils.

A dark forest of lashes blinked over hazel brown eyes several times, and she lifted the pot from the stove before she could clearly see the gravy spilling on her new, blue polyester, and poplin mini skirt. The hot liquid ran like molten lava on the right of her skirt.

"Sweet Jesus, my leg!" her loud, sharp, penetrating cry shot throughout the house. She held the hem to prevent the rest of the scalding liquid burning her leg and bolted like lightening to the faucet to douse her skin.

The pain throbbed and clawed its way from the thigh to the tip of her knee. "Lord, why me, simply because I'm the first born?" Grand mamma passed this cursed legacy to Mamma; the eldest takes over when the mother works outside the home.

She shut her eyes a moment, opened them and stared at a big white blister with a red ring underneath.

Why here? In this kitchen? In this life? Among all this heat, with a fan circulating hot air, a person could get sick. The question kept repeating in her brain. Everything in the kitchen made her sick; the rumples of linoleum, faded kitchen curtains, peeling salad spoons from the wall design, and the double cracked porcelain sink, all caused her an indefinable sense of an ill-being.

Because of the heat and little light from the kitchen window, all of the plants in the kitchen died. She bit her lip to stop tears forming in her eyes. She despised their impoverished condition: the scramble of mice in the walls, the dismal blue faded wall paint, dreary worn carpeting in each of their rooms, the rickety plastic coated beds, kitchen and four bedrooms, the basement with its huge gas water heater, which didn't work properly, and its cold damp concrete floor, made doing laundry there, a distasteful chore. In size and structure, the house was built on legs of brick and cement. Any storm could shake its foundation.

Some day her dreams of going to New York would become a reality, and she'd leave this house and its oppressive boundaries.

"Bill, Tanya, come to dinner," she called, and sat rubbing her leg with olive oil. "Open the oven and fix your food. Start doing for yourselves." Why should she care for a lazy sister and brother, a meanspirited, invalid stepfather, and work a nine to three-job ever day? Tanya and Bill get to rest, and what about her? She loves her family, but should she sacrifice her life? Shouldn't her hopes and dreams become a reality?

Chapter 1

The front door opened and closed as Jennifer limped to the foyer. "Mamma? Hard day?"

"Can't get any worse than this sopping day," Mamma answered.

"After the dry spell, I suppose the flowers needed a drink," Jennifer said. "The ailing mulberry bushes appear stunted and yellow."

"Living proof my good-for-nothing son ain't watered no flowers or cut the grass."

"Don't worry yourself, Mamma. Go to the kitchen and rest." She took Mamma's wet faded raincoat, and water soaked oxfords and socks. "Sit by the oven and dry yourself."

Mamma, lifted her nose in the air and sniffed the aroma. "The chicken smells delicious."

Jennifer limped to the kitchen, prepared a plate of stewed chicken, gravy and rice, collard greens with fat back, and corn bread. She placed the plate in front of Mamma.

Mamma's eyes widened, when she noticed Jennifer's limp. "Lord, today! What happened?"

"I burned myself cooking dinner."

Mamma leaned and lifted her leg. "Does it hurt?"

"Imagine rubbing salt in a wound," she said, and gave a little whimper to accentuate her words.

"Stay off your leg tonight. I'll take Jack's supper to him."

"Thanks, Mamma." Another big headache taken from this day.

Taking care of Mr. Jack is revolting. Curse the day he fell and injured his spine while welding a ship in the Baltimore Harbor. Mamma will support Mr. Jack for the rest of his life, and so will she if she doesn't do something to change the situation.

She listened to the fuss Bill and Tanya made in the living room and it unnerved her. "If you don't get your butts in here—you better. Can you all do nothing besides eating, sleeping and causing confusion? Store the left overs in the refrigerator."

"Dag, Jennifer, I got homework."

"Help your sister, boy." Mamma, pointed her finger at him and sucked her teeth in exasperation. "Make yourself useful."

"Yes, Mamma." Bill tightened his lips and frowned at Jennifer. Mamma gave Tanya a stern look. "Wash the dishes tonight."

Tanya scowled and gave Jennifer a keep-your-mouth-shut glare.

Jennifer gave Tanya a half smile and announced, "I'm going to bed early tonight." She marched to her room, hurled herself in bed and sank in the cold, lumpy mattress.

Hours later, shouting awoke her and she sat straight up in bed. " What a dream!" she said aloud. A loud bang brought her back to reality. "Jesus, Mr. Jack, loves to haul me out of my sleep. Can't Mamma tend to her husband's needs?"

Her one hundred and ten pounds made two of the worn steps creak as she shuffled to the first door at the top of the stairs. "What a nightmare." She climbed the stairs to the second floor in a slow manner, and hesitated a moment. No need to rush in so fast. When she opens his door, he's liable to throw a shoe or anything because of his long wait.

Why sleep on the first level? Can't get far enough away from him? He won't be satisfied till he wears her to a frazzle. She listened outside his room then tapped the door. Don't hear nothing. "Want something, Mr. Jack?"

"Open the door, gal. Hurry! I'm thirsty."

His skinny form arose in bed, and Jennifer squinted going toward him. "Don't see nothing in this room," she declared. That night light

8

makes him appear more emaciated than usual. Must 'a lost more muscle tone, living in that bed for three years?

"Hot night. No breezes blowing through the window," he complained. "This house...so hot...the walls sweat"

"The weather man predicted ninety-five degrees." She raised the vinyl shade higher. "Not a breath of wind is stirring." She tied the dingy, white cotton draperies in a knot, then viewed the wall thermometer. "Eighty-five degrees."

"Hot...always in the summer and cold in the winter." He pushed himself up in bed, and fanned his face with a handkerchief. "Damn brick construction."

She gazed at Mr. Jack's skinny bare chest, then at her mamma, snoring in spite of his noise.

"Don't eyeball me, gal," he said, staring back at her. "Git me the water."

She rushed at the sound of his angry voice and entered the bathroom to run the cold water faucet. When she approached his bed, her intentions of filling his cup and heading back to her room terminated.

"Lazy, you giving me tap water?" His baritone voice echoed through the room, "git the pitcher from the frigid air."

"Yes sir, Mr. Jack." She headed downstairs. Get this, do that...think I'm his personal maid? Got news for him. He'd better enjoy it now 'cause it won't last.

The old refrigerator hummed and she kicked its side. Rusty old junk don't keep nothing cold. Hardly makes ice cubes. She opened the refrigerator and touched the pitcher. Better cool the water with these few pieces of ice. Lord knows she couldn't stand hearing his mouth again.

The ice in the pitcher melted as she hobbled upstairs and handed a glass to him.

He snatched the glass, and spilled half the water on the bed. "You gonna' stand there? Git a towel and fetch a pillow."

She shoved the pillow under his back and darted from the room. "Humph," once in a while, he could say thanks.

9

Jennifer threw her body in bed and tried to get comfortable before she drifted into wisps of sleep, until her alarm sounded. "My God, six o'clock already?" She stifled her alarm, slid out of bed, and into the shower. The warm water washed away her tiredness and the ache between her shoulders. Seven-thirty, she set four plates and the food on the table.

"Morning, Baby," Mamma said and planted a kiss on Jennifer's cheek. "Hmm. Smelled flap jacks all the way upstairs. Made 'em like I taught you."

"Mornings, Mamma, early bird."

"Child, this here's Mr. Charley's golf day. He expects a big breakfast before he hits the balls. Where you workin' today, baby?"

"Cosmetics."

"You might see me. Ms. Hagen loves Sears' cosmetics."

"You driving her, Mamma?"

"Who else? She ain't never gonna put her foot on no peddle again. Mr. Charlie don't stand for her drivin' after she drove on the front yard fence."

"What time? I want to know so I can display the special for her."

"After the cookin', cleanin' and washin. She hurried to finish eating. "Ain't got time for eatin' more 'n one flap jack. Gotta' catch the forty-five bus." She set her plate in the sink and got ready to leave. "Better get them young-uns' outta' bed. Don't need teachers' callin' on the job."

"Yes, Ma'am," she said, going to the stairs and calling to her sister and brother, then, returning to the kitchen to finish eating. "A phone call irritates Ms. Hagen?"

"Les' your folk's dead or dyin', can't nobody talk on the phone but her, and ain't no sittin' in her house neither."

Tanya and Bill bounded into the kitchen, and landed in the chair at the head of the table.

Tanya hit him and he returned the blow to her arm.

"Lord 'a mercy, boy. Wanna' get slap clear into next week? Act a gentleman; take the next seat."

10

"But, Mamma, I get Pappa's chair." He flopped in the next chair, his bottom lip stuck out. "I'm the man of the house now."

"None a' these chairs belong to Mr. Jack," Tanya said. "Because he's bedridden don't make you the man."

"Is Pappa getting well?" He asked.

Jennifer clucked her tongue and declared, "Don't see how, refusing to use his wheelchair, won't get out of bed, won't help himself or take therapy."

"Don't say such," Mamma said. "He gonna' lick that arthritic spine yet."

"Seven-thirty, Mamma." Jennifer shook her head sadly, and thought, Mr. Jack Blade would love to suffer arthritis. From his picture, at age forty, he appeared well built, muscular, with a tiny waist and a stomach one could set a football inside. Not handsome, like her daddy, but his big brown eyes, round clean shaven face, pug nose, and deep honey complexion made him passable. His dazzling smile made his eyes lighten. Now he's a mean old goat, bitter and demanding.

"I can't stay listening to y'all." Mamma dashed to get her raincoat and umbrella. "Remember, on time, for school."

"Yes, Mamma," they sang in unison, waiting for her to leave so they could take their time.

Jennifer prepared a plate of pancakes for Mr. Jack. The way he liked: plenty of syrup, strawberry jam, and two pats of butter. "You all better finish eating by the time, I get back." She carried the tray upstairs and placed it in Mr. Jack's lap.

"Late breakfast again? What took you so long?"

"Got two hands and I used them this morning." Why should she take his nastiness? He never appreciates nothing no matter how hard she tries. "I'm doing my best working alone around here."

He frowned and rolled his eyes in her direction."You an' Martha aught to make them lazy kids help." He raised himself more in bed and gazed at her. "When I ran things, I made 'em, walk the line."

Jennifer's mood changed sharp and angry, and she threw words at him like stones. "If you can do better, get out of bed and do something."

"Smart ass! Getting too big for your britches?"

"I'm eighteen, if you mean my age, and doing my best working inside and outside this house." She gazed at him with loathing, swelling like bile from one's belly. "Your medical bills take money, and I'm telling you my $216.00 a week disappears before I get the check."

A vain in his neck pulsed and swelled. His nostrils flared with fury and he slammed his fist into his opened palm. "You damn, high and mighty little——"

He knew Mamma would hear about him cussing, because she sure would tell her. Taking care of him, when she could go to college, made her react angrily to the challenge in his voice, and she didn't care about hurting him. "Your pension and compensation don't support this family."

Startled hurt turned into red-hot anger. He clenched his teeth and his fury exploded. "You don't know shit about nothing." He almost fell out of bed. "Told Martha about your smart mouth. When your mamma asked about me marrying 'er, you said no."

"She asked for my honest opinion and I answered her." She gasped, and her breath sizzled in her throat. "Get out of bed and use your hands."

He raised himself halfway out of bed. "What the hell can I do with hands?"

"You feed yourself don't you? Use your wheelchair."

His sorrow and self-pity engulfed him, "I live to see the day things don't go as you plan."

Jennifer shuttered at the thought and shriveled a little at his chilled, brittle expression. "If my plans fail, I'll keep fighting till my last breath for plan B." She turned on her heels and stalked out of the room, not turning to see his miserable stare.

"Ms. knows it all," he yelled. "Like to see what you'd do in my place."

"Self-indulgent loser," she yelled back "I wouldn't lay around in bed all day."

She entered the kitchen to find Tanya and Bill arguing over the last pancake. "Move! You heard what Mamma said. Another bunch of losers. Neither one of you like school." Tanya advances to the eleventh grade, Bill to the ninth, only if they finish summer school. "Both of you are going through the motions, not learning a thing."

Tanya peered at Jennifer out of the corner of her eyes, sopped the last piece of pancake in syrup, and stuffed it in her mouth with her fingers.

"You eat like a country heathen. Hurry!"

"We got time to catch the last school bus to Dunbar," Bill said, gulped his milk, then ran to get his books.

"Better get to school if you don't want Mamma's back hand." She pushed them outside, locked the front door, and scurried to New York Avenue to catch the downtown bus.

She caught the bus and reached for a bus transfer to Wisconsin Avenue, hoping to arrive at work before the anticipated rain. Massed black clouds gathered over a few white and brought gusting winds. She knew the weather man could be unpredictable at times and instead of rain, the sun would creep out from behind the blackness to fill the skies with bright radiance that would last all day.

Then maybe, the weather man was correct. She didn't hear the whistling of the Blue Jays or the Cardinals this morning. That's one way that she could tell when it was about to rain; the birds loved to perch on the floribunda tree, outside her window, where they often searched for seed.

When it rained, they stayed away.

She hopped on the second bus before it sped away. This bus, crowded as usual, smells of stale perfume, after shave, and halitosis. She had an attack of nausea and worse standing next to someone needing dental hygiene treatment.

Why did she wear the six inch heels this morning? The three inch stacked ones, from Sears, would've matched her navy blue suit. The corns on her right toes sent hot pains up her legs, and back to her feet, and the muscles in her back ached from the strain of standing. God bless any man who'd give up a seat. Guess we can blame this on women's "lib." Thank God. The next stop was Sears.

She sauntered to her office door, after three blocks, and stuck her key in the lock as Brian, the floor manager, opened the door from the inside.

"Christ, Brian, you frightened the mess out of me."

"Sorry. Wanted to make sure you knew the store hours." He pointed to his watch. "Mr. Timex says, eight-forty."

"Ok. I'm thirty minutes late. The lazy kids at my house held me back this morning."

"You're the top clerk. You should be ready for the customers."

"I'm always ready," she said.

He shrugged, gave her a slight smile and snorted air through his nostrils. "Someone got to keep you on your toes."

She sat on one of the soft, high back, black leather chairs, at the cosmetic counter, and swivelled around to face him with one hand on her hip. "You dogging me?"

"Naw. I'm joking." He sat beside her and locked his hands behind his head. "Your counter is the jazziest in the store."

She relaxed, leaned back in the chair and smiled. "Even when we work together, it's like I'm working alone."

He jumped to his feet. "My Lord, Jennifer, I'll never joke with you again."

"Now, who can't take a joke?" She laughed and slapped his back.

***

Her shift closed at three o'clock. Jennifer glanced at her watch, and her thoughts centered on her sister, Tanya, who had become more of a headache in various ways, especially trying to get her to do any of the household chores. Hope Tanya has done her duty by now. I'm doing no more than cooking tonight. Tanya should do something after she straightened up the night before. She removed Tanya's clothes from her bed room floor: a sweater, a pair of boots, and Bill's books from his floor, folded the clothes she'd washed and stacked them in the linen closet.

When she arrived home, she headed for the kitchen, then strode, to the family room and stood over Tanya.

14

"Breakfast dishes still in the sink? You got something to do?"

Tanya, stretched out on the sofa, watched television, with a cigarette hanging between her lips. She cast an annoying look at her. "Yeah, so? Chill out."

"Don't you think you'd better hop to it?"

She blew the smoke in Jennifer's face. She knew she couldn't stand the smell of cigarette smoke getting in her hair and clothes. "You're interrupting a love scene."

Jennifer ignored her remark and waved the smoke away. "You wash the dishes; I cook."

Tanya's lips thinned with irritation. "Not before my story ends. Do what you got a' do."

Jennifer stomped the floor, her sore back and aching foot forgotten. "Fine! Mr. Jack won't get his dinner, neither you, nor Bill."

"All right!" She didn't want to deal with Mr. Jack. He wouldn't think twice in making her life miserable.

"You know Mamma don't allow smoking in the house."

"Yeah, whatever." She ambled lazily to the kitchen.

Jennifer followed, reprimanding her, "How can you watch stories all evening?"

"My romantic inclination, something you'll never understand, given your high-toned attitude."

"A bunch of nonsense." Jennifer rolled her eyes to the ceiling. "Get a life…some ambition."

"Yeah, whatever." She ran the hot water in the sink, overflowed it with billowing, dollar store, liquid suds, and slapped each plate with the dishrag.

Fatback grease hugged the edges of the sink and pots. Chicken stew, along with the odor of collard greens, sitting around all night with the breakfast dishes, grew and permeated the air.

"Hello, I'm talking reality," Jennifer continued. "You should start thinking about your life."

Tanya tossed her hair, thick, long black and blow-dried, across her shoulder. "I got plans."

"The girl finally got her brain ticking. Which college?"

Tanya batted her eyes. "Oh, boo...or...ring!"

"What then? Success takes plenty of hard work and study."

"Stop messing with me," Tanya yelled. "You earned scholarships and didn't go nowhere. Guess you love D.C. too much, huh?"

"And who would care for Mr. Jack, and help Mamma? Yes, I love this nation's Capitol, but I plan to make something of my life."

"Yeah, sure!" Tanya laughed and threw suds at Jennifer. "You gonna stay in this shack the rest a' your life."

"Lord, forgive this ungrateful girl...calling this house a shack. Daddy built this house with love. He did his best on a bricklayer's salary."

Tanya turned and gulped hard in Jennifer's face, "don't pretend with me. You hate this house as much as I do." Tanya's tears flooded her cheeks and bitterness spilled over in her voice, "Daddy died, then Mamma married Mr. Jack, his buddy, who promised to take care us. He don't care about us."

Jennifer bit her lip to hold back her tears. "A sad day...Daddy's heart giving out. He was always there for us...always laughing, full of fun and gaiety, his warmth and love so abundant."

"He made sure Mamma had everything to spend her days taking care us; we had hot meals to come home to, loving arms to hold us, and comfort, warmth and understanding."

"Don't give up. We can escape."

"Yeah, but not in college." Tanya popped her fingers. " I'm gon a' sing an' write songs."

Jennifer snapped her mouth shut, then smiled behind her hand. " Get real! Your voice won't make you a star."

"Don't matter." With a twist of her head, she shook her hips from side to side, then rolled her stomach. "This will get me in the right doors."

Jennifer's eyes widened, and she tossed Tanya a black layered look. "Girl, what's gotten into you? Better not let Mamma hear your talk."

Tanya threw her head back, sat at the kitchen table and heist her legs in air. "Ever saw a gorgeous pair like them?"

Jennifer couldn't deny Tanya's attractive features: a delicate chocolate face, long and narrow, a thin nose, full lips and an hourglass shape displaying an appearance of a Nubian Princess. Her large brown eyes appeared bitter but bright.

Jennifer regarded Tanya with compassion. "A woman doesn't need a pretty face to get ahead." She took hold of her shoulders, and turned her to face her. "Vulgarity will get you nothing but trouble."

"I'll try whatever gets me out a' this place. So don't sit on your high horse telling me what you think I should do." She scampered back to the family room, laughed, turned the television louder, and deepened her derriere in the torn, faded, blue brocaded sofa.

Jennifer followed her. "I'm not giving in to your stubbornness," she said, shook her head, returned to the kitchen, and contemplated what Tanya said about leaving. Gotta think of a way to get out of this house. Her experience at Sears could land a job at any of the top stores in New York. The extra money could help Mamma, and pay for college.

The idea of going to New York simmered in her head, and when Mamma came home, she met her at the door, took her bag and helped her to the kitchen. "Take a seat, Mamma." She placed a plate in front of her, consisting of pork chops and rice, turnip greens, in fat back, and corn bread.

Mamma stared at her. The lines of fear deepened, a little, along her un-plucked brows and under her eyes. "What's goin' on?"

"I want to get a second job. Make money to go to New York."

Mamma said nothing; acted as if in shock. Then, those ten lines in her forehead deepened, and she brushed her salt and pepper hair back with her rough, water soaked hands. She flashed her large brown eyes, took a deep breath, exhaled, and her fat round face saddened. "I Knew this day was comin'. Didn't expect it this soon."

Jennifer hugged her, and a tremor touched her smooth, marble like lips as she said, "I can't leave you with no help. I won't leave."

Tears welled, Mamma's eyes, and she spoke with broken words, "Wait! Lord knows…I love…Tanya, an' she don't know nothin' 'bout cooking an' helpin' Jack, but she gotta' learn."

She smiled to herself as she spoke, "I'll teach her, Mamma. May I get the job?"

"Course you can. You a wonderful daughter, an' I can't complain. We gonna make out."

Jennifer put her arms around her and broke into an open, happy smile. "Thanks, Mamma."After dinner, Jennifer went to her room to dream. A small apartment would do, maybe in Brooklyn, and later, Manhattan.

Exhausted by her thoughts, she went upstairs to say goodnight and stopped when she heard Mr. Jack's angry voice. She peeped inside the door.

"Why you tell the gal she could work overtime, Martha? You know Tanya won't work."

Mamma raised her voice above his, "we put enough on Jennifer. Time Tanya learned."

"Yeah? Well I ain't a guinea pig," he shouted.

"Jennifer's deservin' of somethin' for herself."

"Notions! Everything goes wrong when women git 'em." He waved his hand as if to shoo, from his mind, the idea of her working overtime.

"She's smart, Jack. With a 4 average, she can make somethin' of herself."

"Got you convinced, huh? Well, she ain't done nothing yet. The gal thinks she better 'n anybody."

"We're her parents and should help her get the rewards from life we didn't get."

"Why should I? She ain't got no love for me."

"Kids love whoever takes care of 'em."

"Who can love kids who don't do nothing?"

"Jack, you know what? I'm tired of your nasty remarks about my kids. You never have nothin' nice to say about 'em."

"When they do something good, then I'll say something nice."

"Ain't anybody taken better care of you than Jennifer. On second thought, go to sleep, Jack. I'll decide about my children."

18

Jennifer closed the door and tipped downstairs, happy that Mamma had confidence in her.

Early, the next morning, Jennifer decided to take a few hours off work to find a second job and after walking through town from one establishment to another, she sat on the steps of Georgetown University Hospital. This was her last stop. Maybe they'd hire her as a nurse's helper.

What if they said no? One way to find out, walk in and ask.

She entered and headed for the employment office. A medium built woman, in a pink dress, peered at her through black rimmed glasses. This lady acts as if she could eat her alive. Better talk fast. "I'd like to apply as a nurse's helper."

The stone faced, woman stretched her dark hair with her hand, and scrutinized her from head to toe. "Have you any experience?"

"I nursed my stepfather for three years. I gave him medicine, his baths, and read his temperature."

"Ever worked in a hospital?" She asked, her expression grim.

"No, Ma'am, but I can learn."

The woman thought a moment and thumped her nails on the desk. "Ok. I'll give you a try. Mistakes are not allowed. Too many can get you fired."

Jennifer rushed to the desk to shake her hand. "Thanks, Miss…"

"Wheatfield, head supervisor," she said, breaking a smile. "Your hours are four to eleven p.m. tomorrow, on time."

Perfect, after her nine to three Sears' Job.

***

Thursday, three p.m., Jennifer rushed to get to Georgetown Hospital. The money wasn't much, $125.00 a week, but she took it home, never purchased anything, and hid it in a sack under her bed. She deposited the money every week. Then one day, she reached for the sack and felt nothing. She lifted the mattress, turned and shook the covers. "Tanya?" She hurried to Tanya's room and opened her closet. "Empty."

She placed a call to the Hagen's house. Mamma answered, and Jennifer bellowed into the phone, "I could kill her. She's gone, and got it all."

"Calm yourself. Take your time. Don't talk fast."

"Tanya got my money and she's run off."

"Naw, she don't know nobody outside us and schoolmates. She'll come home."

"No, Mamma, she took her clothes."

"Wait there." Her voice changed a pitch higher, "I'm comin' home."

While Jennifer waited, her stomach contracted in tight balls, her hands clasped and unclasped in her lap. She bit her nails, as large, crystal size tears flooded her cheeks. She swore, "the little...I'll break her neck." Then she prayed, "Lord, please let Tanya return my money."

Mamma came through the door like a flash of lightening and followed Jennifer to Tanya's room. When she saw the empty closet, she sat heavily in a chair. "Don't worry. Tanya got to be 'round somewhere. Call her schoolmates."

Jennifer called everyone who knew Tanya, and after an hour, gave up.

Mamma went to Jack, "Seen Tanya today?"

"No," he said, acting cantankerous.

Mamma didn't want to admit anything to him, but she couldn't prolong the chance of not finding her. "She's run off."

"I told you she's no good. Crazy gal. Call the po-lees."

"Suppose she comes home? We gonna' look silly and, Tanya upset."

"Suppose we ain't? You going to sit here 'an worry?"

Jennifer knew Jack made sense. She convinced Mamma to call the cops. In a matter of an hour, two burly officers entered and eyed Mamma suspiciously.

The tallest cop began his questioning, "You estimated three hours since missing her?"

"Yes, sir, we called her friends and all her clothes are gone," Mamma said.

"Yeah, she's flown the coop. Got a picture of her?"

Mamma got one of Tanya's pictures.

His straight glance at Tanya's picture, then at Mama seemed to accuse her coldly. "We'll post this with the other missing teenagers."

"Find my little girl. Please, I'm a concerned mother.

Jennifer put her arms around Mamma. "You're the best mother in this world."

The two officers stared at each other, across a sudden ringing silence, and glanced back at Mamma. Derision and sympathy mingled in their glance. "Her age?"

"She turned seventeen this past September."

"We'll find her, if she's still in town."

They left, and Mamma gave in to the built up tension. She doubled over in remorse. " Should 'a talked to her when you told me what she said. Never expected her to run away."

She hated causing Mamma such distress because of the money, but in her mind, she deserved her money.

"Can't see how she's gonna' get far on a few dollars."

Jennifer hung her head. She wanted to keep silent, but she couldn't deceive Mamma. "A year's pay amounted to $6,000.00 dollars."

Mammas' eyes widened. "Lord, today. She's gonna stay a while." She ran a frantic hand over her forehead. "How did she get the money?"

"From a sack, under my bed."

Mamma stared cockeyed at her, unable to believe what she'd heard.

"The rest of the money for my education," she said, avoiding Mamma's bewildered stare.

"You let me down, Jennifer. Tanya got away. What I'm gonna' do now?"

Mamma appeared as if she would slap her, instead, she hit her with a desolate stare. A slap would've eased her guilt.

Mammas' face hadn't appeared this bewildered since Daddy died.

The next day, Jennifer mopped all day at work. Nothing went right. She went about her usual routine at Sears until Mrs. Brown, the supervisor, called a meeting. Jennifer listened with no particular interest, until she mentioned New York. "Our Company in New York needs help for Christmas."

God sent this transfer. She rushed forward, and elbowed her way through the crowd of employees until she stood face to face with Mrs. Brown. "Please, choose me. My life depends on this transfer."

Everyone stopped talking and stared at her. Mrs. Brown frowned. "This job gives you grief?"

Jennifer, embarrassed, sought to clarify her statement, "No...not here...I mean this town. I need a change."

Mrs. Brown laughed and added her name to the list. "Okay, you've got the transfer."

Tears of joy wet Jennifer's cheeks. "Thanks, Mrs. Brown." In the next instance, she was smiling and dreaming again.

Mamma got home early. When Jennifer came through the door, she sat next to Mamma, and put her arms around her. "I got a transfer to New York."

Mamma held her. "I should be happy 'cause the Lord made a way for you, but I'm gonna' miss you."

All pleasure left her when she saw Mamma's face. "I can't leave you, Mamma."

"Hush, child. I'm gonna' make out. Bill can help Jack."

"I'll be here another week. I'll show Bill what to do."

Mamma sounded sad. Tears flooded her cheeks and Jennifer's, too

"Enough! All this sadness. Wipe your eyes. I'm taking all us to dinner next Saturday."

Saturday, Jennifer finished her packing, and Mamma took them to dinner.

"C'mon y'all. We suppose to eat at Phillips' Restaurant."

"We never ate in a restaurant." Bill slapped his hands and rubbed them together in delicious anticipation. "Man, this dinner's goin a' be phat, an' it's goin a' cost."

"Never mind, baby. I saved for this day. Jennifer's goin' away present," she said. "One day you can come back when you make a million and buy us dinner."

They laughed, entered the restaurant and sat at a table near the window facing the Potomac River. A waitress approached their table.

"Evening. My name's Betty. I'll be your server. Y'all want the buffet?"

"Barbecue ribs, potato salad, corn bread and greens," answered Mamma.

"Everything's at the buffet. Anything to drink?

"Sprite, iced tea and coke," Jennifer said.

"You can get started. I'll get your drinks."

The waitress danced off to the kitchen for the drinks, as Mamma, Jennifer and Bill headed for the buffet table. They returned to the table, their plates piled high.

Jennifer laughed and placed her plate on the table. "Wow! Tanya missed a feast."

"Shit. You tight on something?" Bill asked.

Mamma slapped his head. "Boy, watch yo' mouth!"

"Sorry, Mamma. First time she mentioned Tanya in months." He touched Jennifer's forehead. "You sick?

"Why hold a grudge? I'm going to New York."

"Tanya's still a member of this family," Mamma said.

They finished eating and Jennifer called a taxi.

Bill giggled and his giggled faded into a large burp. "Man. My stomach is busting."

"Watch yo' manners." Mamma slapped his head, again. "I'm ready for sleep."

When they arrived home, the phone rang and Jennifer answered, "Blade's residence."

"I'm sorry, I'm sorry," Tanya cried, her voice fragile and shaking.

"Tanya?"

"I 'm gonna make money and pay you every cent I took from you."

"Where you at, Girl? What happened to you?"

"I had to get away...anyplace."

"A selfish pig. Nobody's feelings count...Mamma, Mr. Jack's or mine."

"I've admitted my wrong. I'll pay you back, but I got 'a get a job."

"Why should I trust you?" she asked, in a grudging voice. "Thief. You stole my college tuition."

"Please, Jennifer, don't call me a thief."

A loud noise and screech made Jennifer cover her ears.

"Why you bang the phone in my ear?"

"I dropped the phone," Tanya said in a long audible voice. "Why you think the worse of me? I was desperate. My life was slipping away, in a neighborhood offering nothing to a black woman of my nature."

"Why you calling now?" she asked harshly. "What you want?"

She gave a choked desperate laugh, then answered softly, "I want you to come live with me. We can make it together."

"Let me guess," she added with mock severity. "Your plans didn't work. Now, you want me to live with you?"

"New York can be rough alone. You got brains, know-how. We can work together for both our sakes."

She could save money, and Tanya did owe her. "Ok. Heifer, I'll try your idea, but if you steal anything else from me, I'll get even."

"I've learned my lesson," she said apologetically. "When Can I expect you?"

"I'm leaving tomorrow." She placed the phone on the receiver and called Mamma.

"Tanya phoned. She's in New York and wants me to come live with her."

Joy bubbled in Mamma's laugh and shown in her eyes. "Thank you, Lord. My children gonna' be all right."

Chapter 2

Jennifer's plane landed at La Guardia Airport, and she hailed a taxi.

"Where to, Miss?"

She handed the driver the slip of paper of the address Tanya had given her, when she phoned.

"Abbey Victoria, 151 West 51ˢᵗ Street," he said, into his walkie talkie.

"Never saw such activity. Everybody seems to be in a rush. Is there some parade or important thing about to happen?"

"It's like this every day. Life in the 'Big Apple'."

He stopped in front of the hotel. She got out and handed him a tip, not noticing his huffy manner and angry stance till he threw her bags on the curb.

"I'm sure I'll be able to support my family on this dollar."

"A dollar in hand is better than none at all." She smiled, retrieved her bags and walked inside the hotel. This looks too lavish. She had her mind set on an inexpensive hotel operated by the Calvary Baptist Church. Living in a hotel same as one's religion makes one's safety and comfort.

She rode the elevator to the second floor, got off and used the key Tanya sent, through express mail. "Not bad," she said, aloud, gazing around. "It's not the grand room of the Waldorf Astoria, but more than I expected, and it'll do till I can afford better. Newly pastel painted rooms, including a living room with a wet bar, a refrigerator and a pantry. What more can a girl want?" After inspecting everything, unpacking and arranging her clothes in the closet, she took a shower, got in bed, and waited for Tanya.

Tanya arrived home at eleven. She opened the door and rushed to hold Jennifer in her arms. "You don't know how happy I am to see you. I've missed the family."

"Mamma sends her love," Jennifer said, scrutinizing her. "Now that we've gotten that out of the way, what did you do with my money?"

"I got here, searched for jobs and could find none. I had to pay rent, eat and buy clothes."

"Give me one reason why I shouldn't whip your butt?" Jennifer said.

"I'm working hard," she straightened herself with proud dignity, "washing dishes at Frankie and Lennie's Restaurant to pay you."

Surprise kept her from arguing. "I never figured you for washing dishes."

"Never thought I'd wash none either." She laughed, and hugged her. "You caught hell trying to get me to do the ones at home."

"I'm glad you've realized how hard I worked."

"I regret giving you a hard time," Tanya said. "I'm gon 'a do better."

"That'll be the day."

"You'll see. Give me a chance to prove myself."

They stayed up half the night talking till they got tired. "I've got to get to Sears early tomorrow morning," Jennifer said.

"I don't go to the restaurant till noon. Don't wake me when you leave."

By seven, the next morning, Jennifer hopped out of bed. She wolfed an egg and bacon croissant in four bites, slurped a large black coffee, pulled the blue polyester dress over her head and wiggled to get it over her hips. Then, slipped her feet into a pair of black patten leather heels and ran outside to hail a taxi. When she entered the store, all employees stood at attention in front of the floor manager, and she pushed her way to the front.

26

Her assignment: cosmetics, which would do until she found better. Little did she know her chance would come again, when during lunch break, she found an advertisement in the employment section of the New York Times.

Saks Fifth Avenue? Would she dare? She rushed outside, mingled with the crowd, and hurried along till she came to Saks. Her smile widened. She combed her fingers through her hair and headed for the employment office.

"May I help you, Miss?" said a stout secretary with a fat round face.

Her warm smile gave her confidence and she quickly answered, "I'd like to apply for a job in cosmetics."

"Sorry, all taken. Men's attire is vacant."

"I'd like to apply." Lord, what did she know about selling men's clothing? Maybe the position in cosmetics would become available later. It beats pounding the pavement searching for another job.

After she filled out the application, the secretary directed her to the manager's office. A heavy set, bald man, eyed her for a second, then spoke, "Can you start tomorrow? Nine to five?"

She stared wordlessly across from him, her heart pounding, and finally she said, "I can. Thank you."

Jennifer, left the employment office, joyously unstrained, and enthusiastic. She boarded the bus back to Sears to resign. The manager wasn't pleased. He accused her of using them to get to New York. What the heck, she didn't care. They don't own her and she owed them nothing. They got work out of her since high school.

The next morning at Saks, she stood, smiling at customers, arranging ties in the case behind her counter, and took no notice of a customer until he spoke.

"Excuse me little lady. I wanna' buy all these plaid shirts."

"Yes sir. Would you like blue, green, or red?"

"Give me three dozen each," he said in a loud, husky tone.

He started to laugh, showing most of his teeth. His wide grin, a big bald spot in the top of his head, and his thick black heavy, sideburns, matched his mustache, which covered most of his top lip. He kept his brilliant, black, button eyes fixed on her.

"My name's Joe Morgan."

"Nice to meet you." Jennifer shook the hand he extended.

It took her several minutes to wrap thirty-six shirts. She placed them into four shopping bags.

Joe continued talking, eyeing her as he spoke, "Thanks. My ranch hands gonna' love these."

He walked out of the store, gazed back at Jennifer and smiled. There was something lazily seductive in his look.

What a nerd! Some kind of cow boy. He gave her the willies.

Later that evening, after work, Tanya was sitting before the mirror brushing her hair.

"Got a hot date?"

"No. I'm gon 'a look for a job in a night club. Washing dishes don't pay much and we need an apartment."

"We can stay here till we earn more," Jennifer said. "You can't beat $21.00 a day."

"I know, but I want something of our own."

"Let's wait and scout around," Jennifer suggested. "Something will come our way."

"Yeah, but in the meantime, I'm getting another job. Come with me tomorrow."

The next day, after work, Tanya and Jennifer got a taxi, got out, and stood in front of a blue building with pink lights blinking, and neon girls twisting as the lights blinked. The sign displayed, The Pink Lady Club, and Girls, Girls, Girls.

"Seems like a place just for men," they said in unison. They peered through the window, opened the door and stepped inside. "The lights are brighter outside," Jennifer noted.

They sat at a table near the bar, and noticed several large cages hanging from the ceiling over the bar, some on a small stage behind the bar. Pretty soon a woman came out, wearing a colorful patch over her pelvis and nipples, and got in one of the cages. The woman began to shake and twist her body. Then three others came out, and did the same.

A waitress wearing a short, short skirt, approached. "What you having, Honey lambs?"

"Nothing for me," Jennifer said.

"Uh, let's see," Tanya hesitated.

"What you want to drink?" the waitress asked. When Tanya didn't answer, she started to clear the table. "We need to clean for the next group. It'll be loud and distracting tonight."

"I'm looking for work," Tanya answered. A flicker of apprehension coursed through her, and she appeared frightened and insecure.

"What're we doing here?" Jennifer asked. "You know, darn well, you don't want to work in this place."

"What else can I do?"

The waitress smiled at her and became friendly. "You can make a lot of cash here. How old are you, Sugar?"

"Twenty-one," she lied.

Jennifer's stomach churned with anxiety and frustration, as she eyed Tanya.

"Come with me. You can talk with my boss." She led the way to a little dinky office in back near the bar. "Lane, this little girl wants a job."

A tall, skinny white man with blond hair, stopped counting receipts and turned to look at her, taking in all her bodily dimensions with his small blue eyes. "Can you dance?"

"Yeah, Sir."

He got up, went over to a closet and removed a silver, strapless gown from a hanger.

"Get into this and let me see you."

Tanya took the gown and searched for a place to undress.

"Change in back." He motioned to an entrance draped with a pink curtain and held up by a wooden bar, from where he sat.

Tanya and Jennifer entered the small dressing room with lighted, wide mirrors. Gowns were thrown about, on a couple of straight chairs, before the mirror. She got undressed and tried to fit into the gown. "Too tight." She peered in the mirror and studied herself disapprovingly.

"You look like a stuffed sausage," Jennifer said and shook her head.

After squeezing more into the garment, she wobbled toward the office and stood in the entrance.

"Don't stand there. Closer. Let me see…wow! You're going to pull 'em in by droves." He salivated and drooled. "Come back tonight. You can dance during the second session."

Tanya and Jennifer went back to the dressing room, as the other women entered. "Hi, " said a skinny, redhead woman. "I'm Cindy, the number one dancer."

"Nice to meet you. I'm Tanya. This is Jennifer."

Y'all dancing tonight?" Cindy asked, Pointing at Jennifer and Tanya.

"Not her." Tanya answered. "I'm dancing the second session."

"Welcome," they said in unison.

Tanya and Jennifer sat at the bar and watched the other dancers perform. They started their usual routines. Then Lane came to the bar and beckoned to Tanya and she went over to him. "You're up next," he said.

Tanya got into her gown, went out and climbed on the bar. She stood a moment viewing the crowd. The men in the club whistled and cat called to her. A fat, short man called out, "Come on, babe, show me what you got. Let 'er rip!"

Another man stuck a hundred dollars down her bosom, when she bent down. Before long, Tanya started shaking, while the men clapped and whistled. They clapped harder and louder, and Tanya began gyrating her hips in and out faster till she felt tingling, vibrating motion in her hips, and throughout her whole body. She turned around, bent over and zipped the dress to her hips, showing part of her back.

The men whooped and hollowed and, when she bent over again, she zippered the dress and one of the men stuck five dollars in her bosom. Then, men started flipping more money at her. Tanya had so much money in her bosom that it began to scratch her. When she finished her routine, she hurried off the bar to the dressing room to remove the money from her clothes.

Jennifer followed her. "Give this job the boot. It's degrading."

"Never saw so much money at one time,"Tanya said, not hearing what Jennifer said.

"It's not worth the degradation."

"I need the money," Tanya said, rolling her eyes to the ceiling. In another hour, she went back on the bar to dance and came back again with two hundred dollars. "Never heard of nobody making money like this just exercising."

She made $1000.00 in tips that night, and on the way home, she gave it to Jennifer.

"I don't want shake dance money." Jennifer handed it back. "Don't do this to yourself."

"I've got 'a make a lot of money, and this is the fastest way. We can't stay in this hotel forever."

"It's embarrassing," Jennifer said.

"Can you think of any job that pays as well?"

"Money isn't everything. Please, Tanya."

"It is if we're going to better ourselves." She held Jennifer's hand, "Don't you remember how hard you worked to get money?"

"Yes, but dancing in some God forsaken dive…"

"You got 'a do what you got a' do to survive."

"I don't like you dancing there."

Chapter 3

Tanya worked two months and made $4,600.00 in tips, and $1,600.00 in pay.

"It's pay back time," Tanya, threw the money on Jennifer's bed.

Jennifer's eyes grew wide. "I can't take this money." She gathered it in a bundle and handed it to her. "It's yours. You earned it."

"Ok, don't say I didn't try to pay you."

Jennifer knew the moment Tanya reached for the money that she should forget about her paying what she owed her. She went to work and pushed the episode in the back of her mind.

She was straightening her counter when Joe Morgan returned to the store. "What can I do for you, Mr. Morgan?"

"Would you happen to know where I can hire an experienced housekeeper?"

What's wrong with this man? Do I look like I operate a want ad section? Out of curiosity, she'd find out if he was for real.

"How much are you paying?"

He laughed, louder than a southern gentleman should, and with an almost hopeful glint in his eyes, he answered, "Two hundred a day."

College would come sooner if she could make more money and enough left over to send to Mamma. "Make it three hundred and I'll work for you."

"I can negotiate something." He pretended to hesitate, with his right hand over his chin, resting his elbow on his left hand as though contemplating hard. "Phew! You drive a hard bargain." For a moment he studied her intently, then answered, "Okay, three hundred."

She watched the play of emotions on his face, starring back at her in waiting silence. She thought for a long moment, then answered, "When do I start?"

"Soon as you can pack your clothes. Got a plane waiting at the airport."

His words brought her back to reality. "Where is this place?"

"Lexington, Kentucky. I got a beautiful horse ranch."

"Oh, my God, no! I'm sorry. I plan to attend school."

"You'll have your own room and all that money I mo' pay you."

"I can't."

"Think about my offer. If the answer is yes, I'll wait for you to tell your boss, then Morley, my chauffeur, will drive you home to pack and to the airport."

Oh, perfect. Now she would have to tell Saks that she was leaving. This would ruin her if this turned out to be an old man trying to get into her pants.

Jennifer went home and discussed it with Tanya.

"This could mean money for your education, if you decide to go. Now, I'll have to get another place to stay."

"I haven't said yes. Besides, I don't know this man."

"If you decide to go let me know. I'm going out on the town. Check you later."

***

Tanya hailed a cab. "Take me to some great entertainment."

"We got plenty. Music, art, theaters, dancing, what?"

"Soul music. I wan a' dance."

"Ok. You want the West Boondocks Lounge on 114 10th Avenue."

He stopped in front of the club. Racy sounds of music, laughter and snatches of song filled the night air. She hurried inside. The place jumped to the sounds of some unfamiliar band, but she didn't care. The music made her happy and carefree.

She meandered inside and sat at the bar. "Michelob, please."

"Identification, please."

"C'mon, man. I'm no child?" She leaned forward, swivelled the bar stool, and stretched one long leg before the bartender. "I'm twenty-one for heaven's sake. Gimme' the beer."

"Not without identification."

A tall, dark, muscular man, standing by the door, headed toward them. He stood behind Tanya, peering in the mirror behind the bar, smiling and showing his evenly white teeth.

"Need help?"

Tanya acted like someone in a trance, starring at him in the mirror with her mouth open.

"What's the problem?" He asked.

His oval shaped, chocolate face reminded her of her favorite actor, Billy Dee Williams.

"He's slamming," she whispered, under breath.

"Mind if I sit?" He took a seat, not waiting for her to answer, and waved the bartender away. "It's ok. I'll take care her."

The bartender shook his head and went to the far end of the bar.

"Come with me, I'll get you all the drinks you want." He laughed a full, masculine laugh.

She scarcely noticed her own voice when it became high, "Mamma taught me never to go wit' strangers."

He eyeballed her legs, then her derriere, with typical male appreciation and sheepishly, went back to her face.

"Stranger? Everybody knows me. I'm Nikko Ross." He moved closer. "I got a nice place in Harlem, 125 Street, something like this one."

"If what you say n's true, Mr. Ross, why you here?"

"Scouting for talent," he answered, smiling. "Tell me something, beautiful, you kiss your boyfriend with those lips?" His voice sounded low and seductive.

"No boyfriend. Uh, you looking for a dancer or singer?"

"Both. You know somebody?"

"Oh, my God!" She laughed and slapped her thigh. "Yeah, I sing and dance!"

"When I saw you, I said, this babes got talent." He took her hand, pulled her out of her seat and placed her arm in his.

"I knew the right person would spot me." She smiled a wide smile, and walked outside, her arm in his.

He tore his gaze away from her and placed a call on his cell phone. A long black, Lincoln Limousine stopped beside them. They got in and she snuggled in the large tan leather seat.

"O-o-oh, this is so-o-o comfortable. Never sat in such luxury." She belonged in this car, and with Nikko's help, she could become a star. She rubbed her back against the cool leather. "This car is the bomb."

"My second accomplishment; the club's my first." He poured a drink and handed it to her.

She took a sip, "quality stuff. Never tasted anything like this. My experience with alcohol is an occasional beer with my friends, after school, at their house."

"Glenlivet Scotch, Baby." He poured a shot over ice for himself. "The champagne of Malt Whiskey."

They laughed and drank more scotches before arriving at the club. The doorman for the club opened the car door and Tanya peered at the glitzy sign of fifty light bulbs featuring Eddie Griffin and His All Girl Dancers. She got out and followed Nikko, pushing through the crowd lining the entrance, trying to get inside.

"Eddie Griffin? I saw him on television."

Nikko grinned. "Sure, a night at the Apollo. Eddie's the man."

They pushed their way through the crowd until they got inside.

Tanya looked around. "The stage is large, the dance floor medium."

"This room holds five hundred people." Nikko chose a seat down front near the stage.

"Take a seat, beautiful, enjoy the show."

A waiter brought a tray of sandwiches, a fifth of Glenlivet and a bottle of Mumm's Sparkling Wine.

"I ordered this special wine for you. Drink up, Baby."

Tanya poured a glass of wine and sighed with her eyes closed, "hmm, you know how to live, Nikko."

"You only live once. Why not do it right."

They sat listening to Eddie Griffin' rap and watched his backup singers dance.

"I can do what they're doing," Tanya, danced in her seat. "Nobody ever gave me a break."

"I'll give you one," Nikko said, with a gleam of interest in his gray eyes.

She took a deep breath, punctuated with several low yells, "you kidding me?"

He watched the play of emotions on her face and his eyes sent her a private message. "Tomorrow night, in the club, you sing for me."

Her eyes darted from his face to the stage, and back to his face. "In front of all these people?"

"No. For me, first," he answered. His eyes drinking her up, measuring her with a cool appraisal.

She stared past him, smiling, remembering what Jennifer said about her voice. This audition will prove her wrong. She took several sips of wine and before the night ended, she became inebriated.

"I must say, kid, you can't handle your juice." He took her by the waist and lifted her out of the chair, "I'll take you home. Call me tomorrow when you're sober."

Tanya wobbled inside her room and fell across her bed.

Tanya arose the next morning, before eleven, got dressed and took a cab to Nikko's Club.

She found him seated at his desk in his office counting last night's receipts. "I'm here for my audition." She sat in a chair facing his desk. She wore a black, mini leather skirt, revealing all of her thighs when she sat down. A low cut, white, Lamb's wool blouse revealed half of her large bosom.

Nikko seemed enthralled by what he saw and a mischievous look

36

came into his eyes. He smiled a devilish smile. "Sit your foxy body at the piano." He went toward the bath room. "I'll be out in ten minutes."

Tanya strode happily out and climbed on stage. She sat at the piano.

Nikko came and sat beside her. He positioned his fingers on the piano keys. "What's your song?"

She handed him the paper to which she'd written the notes and lyrics. "You Stepped Out 'a My Dreams."

"You know music?"

Why did she feel she'd just been insulted? "I studied in high school?"

"Well, excuse me, Miss Thang." Nikko played and Tanya started singing.

"When I first saw you, I said, girl you've found your dream. You're my sunshine in the morning and my moonlight in the night. It doesn't matter if it rains cause I got you to hold me tight. You stepped out 'a my dreams. You stepped out 'a my dreams.

I gave you my heart so completely. I thought our love would never end, but when you told me you loved another, my dreams came to an end. You stepped out 'a my dreams. You stepped out 'a my dreams.

I thought you to be special. You seemed to be sincere. You took my love for granted and through my haunting fears, making time with another, and using me to pay your bills. You stepped out 'a my dreams. You stepped out 'a my dreams.

My love for you didn't matter. It became torture to no end. Mama always told me, girl don't be nobody's fool. When there's nothing there to hold you, pack your bags, and let it end. You stepped out 'a my dreams. You stepped out 'a my dreams."

Tanya finished the song and Nikko put his face in his hands.

"I gotta' say this. Baby. You ain't got it."

Crestfallen, her smile quickly faded at the sound of his words. "Wanna see me dance?" Her voice became shakier than she would've liked.

His voice held a note of sarcasm, "hit it, but if you dance like you sing, you're toast."

Tanya unbuttoned her skirt, revealing a hot pink bikini to match her see-through, silk blouse, and a bra under neath. She combined tap, shake dancing, and a bit of break dancing. Nikko stopped playing the piano and studied her. His dark eyes shining with desire and a primal hunger, drinking in the sensuality of her slender physique.

He clapped his hands and rested them on his chin. "Here's what I'm gonna do for you. Feature you in our second show."

A bright flare of happiness danced into her eyes and with a springy bounce, she sat beside him, flung her arms around his neck and kissed him. His lips felt warm and sweet.

This set him aflame and he moved his mouth over hers, devouring its softness. She became shocked at her own eager response to the touch of his lips and pulled away when her lips burned in the aftermath of his fiery passion.

"What's wrong?" He tried to kiss her again.

"Too…a little hot in here," she said, making an excuse to leave.

"Ok. Go to lunch. We'll rehearse your routine later, for tonight."

Tanya became excited about the stage. She's gon 'a be a star. Her own spot. This would show Jennifer and all her friends in D. C. that she had talent.

Nikko ordered two steak dinners and made several calls on his cell phone. "I'm ordering special gowns, one of which, you should wear tonight."

"A gown?" The suggestion intrigued her. "How can I do my routine?"

He stared at her seductively and announced, "you're gonna' sing and strip."

Pains stabbed her heart and a heaviness centered in her chest. "Take off my clothes?" she asked, in a suffocated whisper.

He became annoyed. "Not all. Enough to make the audience want more."

"Aw, I don't wanna', Nikko."

His eyes darkened. He leaned forward and lowered his voice. "Baby. You can't do nothing but a strip. If you strip while you sing, they won't mind your voice."

Tears filled her eyes and she tried to swallow the lump forming in her throat.

Nikko finished eating, but Tanya wouldn't touch her food.

"Eat. We got work to do."

"I'm not hungry."

He noticed the strained tone of her voice. "Cheer up! You'll do well."

Tanya came out on stage wearing a long red sequined gown. A side slit showed red panties, and she wore long, red gloves. The music started and she began singing and dancing around the stage, shedding one glove at a time. Men whistled and cat called, "Come on babe, take it off."

Tanya hesitated awhile, and Nikko gave her a sign with his thumb down. She slowly unzipped the dress to the split, and the dress fell apart around her ankles. She kicked the dress aside and began dancing around, till she finished the song, and danced off stage.

The crowd went wild and clapped for her return. Nikko went back stage. "They want you," he said, smiling. "Put the dress on and do it again."

After Tanya performed her act a second time, she dressed in her regular clothes and got ready to leave. Nikko stood in her path. "I got some friends who's aching to meet you."

"Not now, Nikko, I'm tired," she said, and stepped around him.

He grabbed her by her shoulder and jerked her hard, nearly knocking her off balance. "I gave you a chance, and now, to top it all off, you're annoying me." He ground the words between his teeth. "Do something for me now."

A shutter passed through her and she became afraid. "Ok, I'm sorry, but I can't stay long."

"Do this for me and I'll take care you."

Tanya went with Nikko and he introduced her to two big muscular men dressed in silk suits. The larger man wore a navy, silk suit with a blue gray shirt and tie to match. She didn't like his bald head and thin mustache. He wore a gold earring in his right ear.

The other man wore a brown silk suit, a tan shirt and matching tie.

He wore long braids with a gold ring, and diamond studs in both ears. They grinned when Tanya and Nikko approached.

"Dawgs, meet Tanya," Nikko said. "She's gonna entertain you tonight."

"Nikko, what kind a' entertainment?" Tanya asked, and tapped her fingers against her puckered full lips.

"They got a party going. Dance for 'em like you did tonight."

She'd decided to go along, since it appeared she had no choice in the matter, and she walked out with the two men towering her. They helped her inside a long black Lincoln limousine.

"I'm Cisco," said the one in the blue suit, "an' he's Larry."

Larry smiled and shook his head, looking at her as if he would devour her any minute. He reached over and poured a drink from the small bar and handed it to her with an indulgent wink.

"Lighten up, Foxy. It's cool."

They drove till they came to a development called Jamaica Suites. They got out and entered a red brick townhouse with brown shutters. The room held tan leather couches against four walls, each painted orange, brown, and gold, and a large make shift stage against the back wall. A camera sat hooked up near the stage with a full screen television in back of the stage. Larry looked at Tanya's eyes as they grew wide with apprehension.

"Everything's all right," he said. "We invited people over to watch you and the game I taped between the Nicks and the Celtics."

He went over to a huge console and inserted a tape. The music sounded soft and mellow. He came back to her and took her in his arms. "Dance with me," he said, smiling down at her. She lowered her head and he put his hand under her chin and raised her head, "hold your head high, foxy. Let the men here see your pretty face."

She smiled shyly and raised her head, and he stole a quick kiss. He laughed when she stiffened. "No man ever kissed you before?"

"Plenty of times," she answered, pretending. He held her tighter and pushed his tongue between her lips and she wondered if it felt as good to him as it did to her. Her nerves became so sensitive, and his muscular torso sent pleasures through her body. She experienced an electrifying sensation running through her and she imagined, from the many love stories she'd watched at home, that this was what it was all about. This was called romance.

His hands began to explore her body in a different way. He took her buttocks in his hands and drew her closer, massaging her there. "Ever made love?" he whispered in her ear.

Tanya became anxious. This was all new to her, but she liked and feared the way she responded. "Wait," she said, and tried to pull away. "I'm not used to this. "

"Come on," he said, holding her closer. "Stop kidding."

"No," she answered, and pulled away completely.

"Ok, gorgeous, I won't make you do what you say you're not used to." He let go of her and began preparing for the party. Tanya sat in a chair and waited for the party to start.

Around midnight, others started arriving; a noisy group of men trailed in laughing, joking and boxing each other. When they saw Tanya, they let out a low whistle. "This gorgeous thing's our entertainment?" one of them asked, looking at her as if she appeared to be some mysterious object.

"Grab a seat, dawgs," said, Larry. "This show's about to start."

"Get dressed, baby," commanded, Cisco. "Use the backroom."

Tanya took her gown and hurried to a bedroom decorated in black and white. She sat on the bed and it lowered to the floor, and came back when she got off. A huge mirror covered the ceiling, over the bed, and the Zebra bedspread reminded her of Animal Planet. The dim lights in the black and white lamps on either side of the bed didn't help when she tried to get the zipper, on her gown, unstuck.

The music started, she hurriedly zipped her gown and entered the room. Rhythm and blues blasted from the massive speakers. She began to bump and grind, taking off one glove then another, tossing one into her audience. When she unzipped her gown, she did so sensuously and slowly until she danced in her bikini set.

"Let it flow, honey, let it flow," someone yelled.

Tanya discovered a brand-new joy. They clapped for her. She made them happy, and she laughed and kicked her shoes off, as she finished her dance. One of the men grabbed her shoe, poured champagne inside and drank.

Larry took her home at two o'clock a.m. "You did great tonight," he said, poking her nose with his finger.

"My pleasure, sir," she said, smiled and closed her door.

After Larry left, Tanya fell in bed, exhausted by the events of the night and the fact somebody liked her.

***

Tanya spent the next night with Nikko. "I heard great things 'bout you, baby." He drew her close and hugged her. "You did me proudly."

"Nothing, but fun, Nikko."

He grinned at her. "Told you."

"Yeah, Thanks," she said, grateful the men at the party didn't get as wild as she expected.

"My best friends," he said. "We hang together."

"How long have you known those guys?"

"Since high school," he answered, and pulled her down on the couch.

She arose from the couch, but Nikko mistook her intentions. He pulled her back on the couch. "No," she said. "Don't touch me." She tried to leave, but Nikko held onto her.

"What's your problem? You a lezzie? Lay it on me."

"I never made it with guys. Please, don't be angry with me."

"If you for real, I'm not angry." His burning eyes held her. "But if you shit tin' me…"

"I'm not, Nikko."

He threw his head back and roared with laughter. "You the first stripper I've hired with a cherry."

She couldn't help herself as she laughed loudly, and removed his apartment key from her key ring.

He took the key and gave her a pat on the behind. "Get ready. It's Tanya time."

She did a little dance and scurried from the room making him laugh.

Tanya stayed in the dressing room getting ready for her act. The other strippers entered. Patty, the older stripper, came over and sat beside her. "How about Nikko's latest conquest, girls?"

The others began to snicker as Patty continued harassing Tanya. "Heard she got to do all his friends the other night."

Anger coursed through Tanya's body and she exchanged an exasperated look with her. She took a deep breath and narrowed her big brown eyes to thin slits. "Just what in the hell do you mean?"

Patty faced her with a mocking smile and stated, "you know, honey, his working slut."

Tanya looked Patty straight in the eye. "It takes one to know one, but in this case there's only one, and it's not me." She headed for the door and called back, "Oh, by the way, I heard you did all of Nikko's friends."

They all rocked with laughter and Patty threw a shoe at the door behind Tanya.

***

Tanya and Nikko grew closer and closer. They ate dinner together every night and he took her shopping on Saturdays. Patty became jealous and looked for ways to destroy their friendship. One night, she got Nikko alone in his office. "I've heard very much about your prized hussy."

"What the hell are you crabbing about now?" Nikko asked, half listening to her.

"Ask your friend, Cisco," she said, and laughed.

Nikko got his cell phone and called Cisco. "What happened at the party, dude?"

Later in the evening, after Tanya finished her routine, Nikko called her in his office.

"I got another favor to ask of you, baby." His eyes appeared flat, hard and hateful.

"Something wrong, Nikko?"

"Naw. What could be wrong?" A faint glint of fire lit his eyes. "I got another party for you."

Her eyes brightened with pleasure, she smiled and answered, "ok, fine, Nikko."

"Meet me here at 11 o'clock tonight."

Tanya did as Nikko said and she waited for him. He came to his office with a big, muscular guy; short braided hair, smooth shaven and dressed in a red leather jacket and black pants. He reminded her of some of the wrestlers her brother watched on Saturday night television.

She sensed an odd feeling about this one. Something isn't quite right. "What kinda' party is this, Nikko," she asked, scrutinizing the man.

"The same as last time. This is Daniel. You go along with him."

"Oh, man, you're killing me, Nikko."

"This is the last time I'll ask you."

Tanya got into a red Corvette and Daniel took her to the Westchester Marriott Hotel. They got off on the fifth floor and entered the living room. "You can change in the bedroom," he said, his burning eyes raking over her. "Expect three other guys."

Tanya heard the music start and grow louder. She undressed, lay her gown on the bed, and removed her pepper spray from her purse. "A girl can't be too careful," she said aloud, and positioned the spay between her thighs, in her underpants. In the next instance, the door opened.

"I'm not ready yet," she said, holding the gown in front of her.

"Oh, you're ready, whore," Daniel replied. He pulled the gown and tossed it to the floor. "We'll play musical bed first."

"No, please, Nikko don't want this." She knew she couldn't fight him. He outweighed her by a hundred and forty pounds. He threw her on the bed and straddled her. His lips parted, trying to join their mouths. She tried to scream, but his mouth closed over hers.

She reached for the pepper spray and went for his eyes. His screams sounded like a scene in a murder mystery as he ran to the bathroom.

Tanya got into her clothes, and raced out of the building. What happened? Why did Nikko do this to her? She trusted him. Tanya came out to leave when Nikko's car stopped beside her. He got out and she confronted him. "Nikko?" she cried, tears streaming down her cheeks."You wanted him to hurt me?"

"I'm sorry! Cisco told me Larry got a little."

"He lied. We didn't have sex."

"Cisco said you played me for a fool." His face took on a tortured stare as he peered into her eyes. "I'm sorry this happened." He led her to his car and she sat huddled near the door, away from him.

When they reached her hotel, he helped her out of the car and she jerked her arm away. "I don't wan 'a see you no more, Nikko."

"I don't blame you." He shot her a twisted smile. "Take this money. It's a thousand dollars."

She frowned and threw the money in the street. "I'm not your whore."

He bent down, gathered the money and got into his car.

Tanya got to her room, hurried to the shower and scrubbed her flesh with all her strength.

Chapter 4

Jennifer went to the bathroom and saw Tanya on the floor in the shower. "What happened?"

"I wan 'a die."

"Don't say that." She helped her to bed, and forced her to tell her about Nikko. "You got to report him?"

"Who would believe a stripper?"

"Those bastards aught to pay for what they did to you." She clenched her hands and pounded her chest. "I want to make them pay."

"We can't," she said, and curled into a fetal position. She lay there all night not falling asleep till dawn.

Three days later, she got out of bed. "I can't stay in the hotel another day without getting a job."

"Go back to Frankie and Lennie's."

"Yeah, they still need a dishwasher. I can do that."

"I'll go with you. Lend my support."

Jennifer and Tanya got a cab and went to the steak house. Mr. Alonso was standing there, scratching the bald spot in the top of his head. When he noticed Tanya, he scowled.

"What do you want?"

"My job."

"Why should I give you another chance? You left without proper notice."

"C'mon. You need a dishwasher," her soft voice implored him. "I'll work hard every day."

He narrowed his eyes. "Ok. I'll give you another chance. Come with me." He took them to the kitchen.

Jennifer and Tanya stared at all the dishes on the long wooden rack moving through a tunnel of water.

A tall skinny black girl tossing salads nodded her head and whispered through her lips, "It's not bad."

"Yeah. I can do this."

"Ok," Alonso said. "This is Louise. Get acquainted."

"Don't worry," Louise said, shaking her hand. "How many people you think know what they're doing on the first day of a new job?"

Tanya gasped. "I worked here a year ago and left. I made a mistake. Wanted the big time."

"Not to worry. I'll help you."

When Louise didn't prepare salads, she helped Tanya with the dishes. She showed her everything about cooking and making special dishes.

"I got my job. You and Mamma will be proud of me."

"We're proud, Tanya. You've learned from your mistakes."

***

Joe Morgan entered Saks and headed for Jennifer's counter. "I have to return to my ranch. Are you working for me?"

"I'll take the job and if it doesn't work out, I'll come back."

When Jennifer got home, she told Tanya of her decision, "I'm leaving for Kentucky."

"I'll have to get a roommate or another apartment. Louise asked me to move in with her."

"We can both leave in a few days," Jennifer said.

"Louise won't mind you staying till you leave."

The next day, Tanya and Jennifer paid the bill at the hotel, packed everything and were waiting when Louise honked her horn. She and Jennifer loaded all of their stuff in Louise's S U V.

They rode for twenty minutes, then, Louise stopped and parked the car in the drive of a small, beautiful, blue and white wooden bungalow with gray shutters. It was landscaped with Texas yaws around the edge of the porch and a tulip poplar tree on the lawn.

Louise, opened her door, and lead them to a medium sized room done in pink. "Welcome. It's not fancy but it's clean."

"She's right," Jennifer whispered. "The furniture isn't expensive, just average. Nothing like our rooms at the hotel."

"If you want to stay here, you can pay me a hundred bucks a week," Louise said. "Food 'll cost another fifty."

"Thanks," They said in unison.

Louise left them and went to her room.

Tanya and Jennifer got undressed and went to bed. Tanya slept until ten the next morning, but Jennifer left early to go to work. Tanya was about to get out of bed when Louise knocked on the door.

"If you want breakfast, you fix your own. Pay me when you get your check. Got to go out now."

Jennifer gave Saks her notice. Mr. Anderson, the manager, folded his arms across his chest and gazed at her as if he wanted to strangle her.

"Can't you finish this week out? There's no one to man your counter."

"Sorry, my new boss wants me to leave tomorrow."

He shoved his hands into his pockets and gave her an evil eye.

"I hope you know you'll never work here again." He kicked the door closed before she could respond.

"Boy. He was mad with me," she said aloud.

Jennifer went back to the house, packed all of her clothes and called Mr. Morgan. Mr. Morgan arrived in a big black Lincoln limousine. "This is Morley. He'll help with your bags.

Jennifer and Tanya hugged for a long moment, then, Morley threw the bags in the trunk, helped her in the car and sped off like a race car driver.

When the car neared the airport, Morley slowed and stopped. Joe helped Jennifer out and they entered a two-engine private plane. The plane taxied down the runway and Jennifer held onto her seat. Joe laughed and took her hand in his.

"Open your eyes. Don't be afraid. I'm here."

Jennifer didn't bother looking out because she closed her eyes all the way to Kentucky. She peered out of the window when Joe called out, "Welcome to Kentucky and Blue Grass Field Airport, darling."

A few men dressed in blue jeans and red plaid shirts stood beside a light, blue Lincoln Continental, waving and yelling. Joe waved back and led Jennifer off the plane to the waiting limousine.

"See how my ranch hands love me?" He boasted and waved with both his hands.

Morley ran ahead and got into the driver's seat of the limousine, and the ranch hands walked off to a red, Ford pick up truck. An hour later, Morley drove through an open black iron gate with a wroth iron sign painted in large red letters reading, "Green Valley Farms." They stopped in the winding drive of a large beige, brick house with black shutters. A tall white picket fence surrounded the house.

Jennifer shaded her eyes from the bright sun to stare at the luscious Kentucky landscape.

"Did you loan this land to the movie industry for their western movies?" she teased. "It's perfect."

Joe chuckled, and stated, "Rolling hills, thick velvety bluegrass and miles of white board fencing." He took her hand and helped her out of the car. "Come with me." He led her around the side of the house to the stables. "Each stall is painted in different colors of orange, red, blue, and green."

Thoroughbreds and quarter horses snorted and tossed their heads as Joe and Jennifer walked by their stall.

"Ever been up close with a horse before?"

"Can't say I ever," she said, mimicking a southerner.

Joe brushed one of the thoroughbreds and pitched it some hay. "This here's Mystic Knight, Black Pearl, Silver Lady, Wind Spirit, Moon Star and Priceless Bow." He patted each horse and gave them a kiss. "They've all been stars at the Derby, the Preakness and Belmont. Now they're studs. Just waiting to give and produce prize colts."

"They're beautiful and everything is so clean."

"Wait till you've seen inside the house. You get to pick your room of twelve bedrooms, mine included." Joe laughed, deep and loud when he noticed Jennifer's red face.

Jennifer's delicate eyebrows lifted, and she released her fingers from his; her coolness evident that she was not amused. In fact, she became afraid and backed away from him.

"I don't sleep with men."

"C'mon, I'm joshing with you." He laughed and took her hand in his again. "How old are you?"

"Twenty," she answered.

"Don't be so serious about everything."

They left the stables and entered the house. "It's like a story book palace. Shiny floors... like one of Mamma's clean dishes."

Joe laughed, his voice loud and hearty. He took her shoulders and turned her toward him.

"I like your description a' things."

Jennifer become embarrassed, especially when he continued to laugh, as he led her upstairs. When they entered the first bedroom, facing the top of the stairs, a flicker of apprehension coursed through her.

He beckoned to her, and added in a lower, huskier tone, "Enter. I'm not going to jump your bones."

Jennifer stepped inside, her feet sank into a blue and white, plush carpet, where in she kicked her shoes off and walked around the room, enjoying the softness of the pile. Then, she walked over to the queen-sized bed and ran her hand over the baby blue, silk bedspread, and peered out of one of the two windows on either side of the bed, admiring miles of blue grass, manicured and cut to look like a carpet.

"Magnificent. I've never seen nothing like this, except in the movies."

"Don't stop here. We got eleven rooms to go."

She looked at the high domed, white ceiling with stained oak beams. "I'd like this room."

"Okay." He nodded his head and went down stairs.

After Jennifer settled in her room, she planned her daily routine, and, by the weekend, she got half the house in shape.

All the ranch hands and Joe finished their work and wanted to go into town, 'live it up', they called it.

Joe knocked on Jennifer's door. "Time for fun. Let's go to town."

"Thanks for asking, but I'd rather stay here."

"Nonsense. Everyone leaves the ranch." He opened her door and entered her room.

Her lips puckered in annoyance. "I've nothing to wear."

"That ain't a problem. We'll get you some new duds." Joe whisked Jennifer in and out of several shops; trying dresses, jeans and shirts, selecting a few of everything, including a dress she particularly adored: a blue flowered, gingham with ruffles on the off shoulder, bordered neck and hemline, which she wore, instead of changing back into her old clothes.

Joe took her to lunch, and they dined on barbecue ribs and potato salad, then onto the Kentucky Horse Park; where he explained the activities surrounding the day-by day care of the thoroughbreds. They watched a horse pulling contest.

"No one ever spent time with me, as you've done today. Thank you."

"My pleasure. It's all in fun. Now, let's wrap it up by taking a ride with me to the hospital."

Out of Concern, Jennifer's expression changed and grew serious. "Are you sick, Mr. Morgan?"

He gave one of his slow secret smiles, before answering, "No, I want you to take a blood test."

Her lips parted in surprise, and she stated, "I'm in good health. I'm never sick."

A suspicious line formed in the corner of his mouth, as he lied, "It's required of all my employees." He took out his beeper and signaled Morley. The car pulled along side of them. "Take us to the hospital."

Joe and Jennifer got their blood drawn, and when Morley took them back to the ranch, she went to her room and waited for Morley to bring the packages containing her new clothes. She gave no thought to what took place this day, other than Joe taking her shopping and all the pretty clothes hanging in her closet.

***

Joe reserved the mansion at the Marriott's Griffin Gate Resort in town, and he went to Jennifer's room to tell her. "Have you forgotten what day it is?"

"Is it something special? She asked, looking puzzled and dumbfounded.

He leaned forward and exclaimed, "Dang, it's your birthday!"

She yelled, her voice sliding up a scale. "I clean forgot," she said, talking like one of the ranch hands.

Joe laughed and said, "Let's take a run into town. Got a special party planned. Wear your prettiest dress. Gonna have a tough time keeping men away from you." He had watched her develop into a beautiful woman, with a figure like a coke bottle. Her legs were still slim, her bust well developed and her large, almond-shaped brown eyes were brighter. All of the ranch hands eyed her, but at the same time, respected her. None tried to get fresh with her. He realized, with all certainty, that respecting her meant everything to him. He had to protect her and be there for her, because she needed him.

That evening, all the hired help was invited to the party. Joe and Jennifer arrived and entered the mansion first. Joe looked to see if everything was as he had ordered. The room was decorated in green with yellow linen tablecloths and green napkins shaped like sailing ships. The orchestra began playing rhythm and blues. Joe patted his foot.

"Everybody, get up and dance. Have fun," he commanded. "We're gonna make Jenni happy tonight."

Two waiters, from the hotel's Pegasus' Restaurant, rolled in a huge cake with green and white icing, yellow candles and a large number 21 in the middle of the inscription; Happy Birthday,

Jennifer. Joe started singing happy birthday and Jennifer blew out the candles. She laughed and said, "Thank you, Mr. Morgan."

"Joe to you, darling. Only you can call my name." Then he clapped his hands and commanded, "Champagne. We're gonna toast this little lady," he spoke to all, but gazed only at her.

The waiters brought bottles of Mumms' Champagne to every table. When they were about to pour Joe's wine, he seized the bottle and poured a glass for Jennifer. "Here, darling, you get your first drink."

Jennifer raised the glass to her lips and took a sip. "It tickled my nose." She laughed gently, and took another sip.

"More!" he said, filling her glass to the rim.

Jennifer drank till she'd had four glasses of champagne. "My head is big…funny," she said, laughing. "The room is a merry-go-round."

"Hear that?" asked Joe, laughing. "She makes everything sound so emphatic."

Everyone laughed, and Joe kept filling her glass. Soon, without her knowledge, she had fallen out at the table. "Hot doggedly! C'mon, pretty one. Joe's gonna take care you." He picked her up in his muscular arms, and carried her to the car.

Morley followed. "I'll get her home in a jiffy, sir."

"Never mind home. Drive to Judge Warp's house. This little gal's gonna be my wife."

"Sir?" A frown creased the corners of his dark, puzzled eyes.

"You heard me. Step on it."

"Yasser," Morley said, and drove faster than his usual speed. When he stopped, he was in front of a large red, brick house. Joe got out of the car and carried Jennifer up to the door. He banged on the door with his fist and yelled, "C'mon, get up. I wanna get married."

The housekeeper came to the door. "Who's making this fuss? Don't make no kinda' sense. Folks trying to sleep."

"Never mind sleeping. Wake the judge."

"Mr. Morgan? Didn't recognize you, sir," she said, softening her tone. "Come on in. I'll get the judge."

A few minutes later, which seemed like an hour to Joe, Judge Warp entered the room wearing his robe and slippers. "What's going on, Joe? Why you all fired up?" He rubbed the sleep from his eyes and looked at Joe for some explanation till he smelled his breath. "Why don't you go home? Sleep it off and come back tomorrow."

"I promised this little lady I was gonna take care 'a her," he said, raising his voice in Judge Warp's face. "Get your preaching book."

"Okay! Calm yourself," Judge Warp urged and moved away from Joe's breath. "I'm getting my bible."

The judge came back into the room and Joe stood holding Jennifer. She mumbled, "No," in a low, slurred tone.

Judge Warp looked up from his bible. "You sure this girl wants to marry you?"

"Said so, didn't I? Git started."

"Whose going to answer when I ask, do you take this man for your lawful wedded husband?"

"She'll answer. Go 'head. Forget the fancy stuff."

Judge Warp began, "Do you, Joe Morgan, take this woman to be your lawful wife, to love, honor, cherish and obey till death?"

He answered, loudly, "I do!"

"And do you...what's her name?"

"Jennifer," Joe yelled.

"Jennifer...take this man to be your lawful wedded husband to love, honor, cherish and obey till death?"

"Say yes, my darling," he shook her, and held her tightly.

"No," she moaned.

"She means yes," Joe assured him. "Had a bit too much to drink."

Judge warp looked at him sideways, as if he didn't believe him, but asked, "Where's the ring?"

Joe took his diamond ring off his little pinky and put it on Jennifer's third finger.

"I now pronounce you husband and wife. Kiss the bride."

"That'll come later. I'm taking my wife home. He threw fifty dollars at Judge Warp, whirled Jennifer around and around. "I got me a bride!" He hurried out, and shuffled her into the car. "Get us the hell home, Morley."

54

"Yes sir." Morley took off like a fired cannon ball. He got them home in less than forty minutes.

Joe carried Jennifer to his bedroom, undressed her and laid her on his bed. Then he got undressed and in bed next to her. He kissed her neck and her lips. She couldn't miss the musky smell of him as he pressed her closer, and she tried to push him away, but she wasn't strong enough. Then, a warm, moist pressure on her right nipple; a soft sucking motion, and a rough hand kneading her small, thin hips, sent a pulsing knot in her stomach.

He turned her on her stomach and she gave a low moan. In the next instance, he fumbled with her mound, then the weight of his large frame on her back, and a thrust of hardness within her, brought a burning sensation to her genitals.

While he panted, pushed and battered, she tried to move, but the weight of his stomach in the small of her back prevented her. She lay there through the whole ordeal of sweat, stale liquor, chewing tobacco, a slobbering tongue and his body consuming hers till he grew limp, and his heavy torso raised and rolled on his side of the bed.

"Come, darling, we'll shower together." He took her hand and lead her to his bathroom.

Jennifer stood naked in the glass enclosed shower not moving or saying anything while Joe soaped her body and rubbed her with bath oil like a new born baby.

After they showered, Joe helped her into her pajamas, and tucked her in bed. She was exhausted as she turned on her side and dropped into a fitful sleep.

Jennifer awakened, the next morning, "My head. My stomach. Did I eat some of Tanya's cooking?" Her eyes widened and wandered around the room. The white ruffled curtain at the window, on her side of the bed, wasn't hers. The blue carpet, the cherry-wood dresser, with the blue ceramic lamp, wasn't there the day before.

She looked at the tall bed post, threw the covers aside, jumped out of bed, and ran to her room. She hurried to the shower, but no amount of water or soap washed the horror of him off. Confusion and embarrassment swept over her. Her heart pound her ribs as she tried to remember. How did she end up in his bed? Did he put something in her drink? She held her throbbing head with both hands. Then she remembered. "The champagne!" How could she have been so stupid?

Joe, awakened, and ran his hand on the side of the bed where Jennifer had lain. When he didn't feel her beside him, he tumbled out of bed and ran down the hall to her room. "Darling," he called through her door.

"Go way, please," she begged, her voice barely audible.

He knocked. "Open the door. It's all right. Were married."

His words siphoned the blood from her face. She fell on her hands and knees. "You're lying! Oh, please, dear God, say you're lying."

"No. You're my wife."

"I don't want to be married." Hot, scalding tears flooded her cheeks, and she lay on the floor and sobbed until exhaustion overcame her.

Joe listened to her crying and tried to console her, but made it worse. "Now, darling don't get upset. You'll get use to married life."

"I'll never get use to being married to you." Her voice was suddenly firm and much stronger. "This isn't what I planned for my life." She lied there and her thoughts lingered back to her beginning: how she fought to get to New York, how Mr. Jack kept her from getting everything she wanted, and Tanya taking her money. Now, Joe, had become her enemy, and she hated him more than she did Mr. Jack.

"C'mon, Jenni. You're suffering from a hangover. You'll feel better after breakfast."

"Leave me alone," she yelled. "I don't want nothing from you ever."

Joe became impatient, "Ok, open the door. I got a key, but I'mo give you the chance to open."

Sheer, black fright swept through her, and she shivered, as the fearful images of what happened to her during the night flooded her memory. She put a chair under the door knob as he tried to open the door, pushing and kicking, but he couldn't.

"You got to come out someday. You can't stay in there forever," he said, his voice hoarse with frustration. "I'll wait."

She heard him storm down the hall, and she took a seat by the window, where she stayed all day devising a plan to remove herself from her nightmare.

Joe posted his adopted son, Little Fox, outside her door. He was big, as a grizzly bear. According to Joe, a full-blooded Tarascan Indian, whom he'd rescued from Lake Patzcuaro, in Mexico, when he was six years old. Joe brought him home and raised him. He worshiped Joe, and the ranch.

She was a prisoner, but she held steadfast for three days, her only nourishment, water. She lost three pounds, and she failed at every attempt to get away from Joe. She'd escape, no matter how long it took. "This has got to stop," she told herself, got out of bed and marched past Little Fox, who had fallen asleep but stood the moment she came out of her room. His hawk eyes followed her and he turned back, when he spotted Joe in the den, reading his newspaper. Jennifer stood in front of him, her heart cold and still. "Joe?"

He dropped the newspaper and gazed at her.

"I'm not ready to do what you think I should." She stared him in the eye. "I'm at an unfair disadvantage."

A tired, sadness fell over his features, and he said softly, "I married you because I wanted to care for you."

"I never asked you. I've been taking care of myself since I was ten."

"You got me now," he said, "you needn't worry."

A painful flutter arose at the back of her neck, and she tried to ignore the strange aching in her limbs. Her mouth throbbed with an imploring message, "please, let me go."

He blew her a kiss, and went to the stables.

She felt her pulse beat in her throat, felt it racing through her bloodstream. I've got to get out. She opened Joe's desk drawer and removed stationary and a pen. She began a letter to Tanya, telling her about Joe and their marriage. She finished the letter promising to contact her later. She placed the letter among his stacks for Morley to mail.

During dinner, a tense silence enveloped the room. Jennifer poked her food while joe finished his. Out of concern, he spoke to her. "If you don't eat more, you gonna' get sick. I'd better get Doc. Millers for you."

Oh, no! He'll spoil her plan "No. A doctor can do nothing for the flu. I need a couple of days."

"Ok, otherwise, I'mo call 'im."

He bought her story about the flu. Now she had to plan her escape. She lay in bed thinking of how her life changed, she'd married a man she didn't respect or love, a man fourteen year's older. He cheated, lied, and deceived her. She wanted marriage, but in time; to a man around her age, and she wanted a church wedding with lots of flowers, brides' maids and her brother walking her down the isle. Joe ruined everything.

Joe become impatient, especially since his ranch hands and house servants ribbed and whispered about him. One evening, after he'd gone to the race track, he came home sloppy drunk, the term her Mama used for someone who drank till he could no longer stand. He refused to let Morley put him to bed, and he banged on her door. "Jenni, open up! It's time you give me what's due."

"Go away, Joe. We'll talk in the morning."

"No! Now, damn it. I'm tired of excuses." He tried to unlock the door, but she had gotten Bobby Rae, one of the ranch hand, who disliked what was happening to her, to put double bolts

on the door. Earlier, that day, Bobby Ray had finished the job and placed a bag in her hand. "Here, Ms. Jennifer, you might need this."

She removed the contents in the bag. "A gun? No, I don't need a gun."She handed it back.

"It never hurts to pack some iron, Ms. Jennifer."

"You could be right." She placed the gun in the dresser drawer "I'm a' put something' else in this house for you, too."

Jennifer nodded her head, not paying particular attention to what he'd said. She was afraid to ask what else he had planned for her safety, but she was happy with the locks because now, Joe couldn't get in her room. He kicked the door and cursed her, before he stumbled to his room.

The next day, Joe didn't come to breakfast, lunch or dinner, nor did he bother her. She stayed in her room watched a movie about young girls employed as striptease artist in a night club. She thought of Tanya, and an idea of escape. Why not? Everything he owns is as much hers as his.

Chapter 5

"I'll slip away tomorrow night," she muttered as she continued to watch. "Everyone is tired and drunk after work. That's the day of round up." Joe always allowed the men to drink and have a good time. Nobody would guard her 'cause they'd all pass out.

That next day, she got up early, packed her clothes, hid the suitcase under the bed, then went to breakfast. Joe didn't say anything to her, nor she to him. Later that night, she waited in her room till everyone had retired, and around midnight, she opened Joe's safe, removed $75,000.00, got her suitcase, and sneaked past a Little Fox, who had passed out on the floor. She made it to the highway, waited till a truck came along and frantically stepped in its path.

The truck skidded and stopped a few feet from her, and a tall, slim, man jumped out and ran toward her.

"What's wrong with you, lady? A few feet more and you'd a been mince meat."

"I'm sorry," she said, taking his arm, hurrying him to his truck. "I've got to get out of here."

"Somebody chasing you?"

"Yeah!" She peered into the darkness, in the direction of the ranch. "Please, I need a ride."

"He hurriedly helped her into the truck. "Where're you headed, Ms.?"

"Anywhere." She sat a moment and tried to pull her drifting thoughts together. Then, she said, "Drop me by the airport."

"Airport?" He shifted in his seat. "I ain't going that way, lady."

"Please. I'll pay."

"What happened to you?"

She searched for a plausible explanation, "I quit my job and my boss got angry," she answered without hesitation. She felt him staring her down, perhaps it was her own uneasiness, but she refused to think that he would harm her. He was curious, like all the other men she'd encountered around the ranch.

"Ok. I'll drop you."

"You're saving my life."

Jennifer gave the stranger a hundred dollars, got a ticket to New York and after she landed, took a taxi to Louise's house.

"Your letter made my heart sink," Tanya said. "I cried for you."

Jennifer talked for twenty minutes, telling her story to Tanya and Louise.

They listened with dazed exasperation, then started yelling.

"Make that bum pay through the nose, "Louise said and gritted her teeth.

"Yeah, take him for all he's worth." Tanya added.

"I have enough for what I plan to do. We can't stay here. He'll have his men searching for me."

"I've enough to strike out on my own," Tanya said. "I don't plan to make this my life's work."

"Better not let him catch you," Louise warned. "From your description of him, he'd hurt you on the spot."

"I saved sixty thousand dollars, and I'm ready to leave," Tanya disclosed.

"Buy a ticket somewhere far away, 'cause if he catches you, it won't be good."

Jennifer paid little attention to what Louise said about Joe. Her face was full of strength and shining with steadfast determination. "If you wanted to get away, where'd you go?"

Louise closed her eyes and said, "California! That's where everything's happening."

"Yeah! I've always wanted to go where those movie stars live," Tanya said. We're headed straight for the sunshine."

"Okay, I'll drive you to the airport, and I won't know anything when Joe comes searching for you."

"We want two one- way tickets to Los Angeles." Jennifer stated. Before boarding, They kissed Louise goodbye.

When the airplane landed at Los Angeles International Airport, Jennifer hailed a taxicab. "Take us to a moderately priced hotel," she told the driver.

"Do you want glitter?" he asked

"Not where We'll get lost in the shuffle," she answered.

The driver took off and stopped in front of the Las Angeles Hilton.

"Here we are. The Hilton's a mini city: casinos, entertainment, café, bars, restaurants…you name it."

Jennifer paid the driver, got out and went inside to register. She got a room and a newspaper.

"Got 'a find a place to invest my money,' said Tanya, as she scanned the want ads.

"While you find your niche, I'm going to visit the University of California."

"Follow your dream, Jennifer, baby, cause I'm shore gon a' find mine."

Tanya viewed every page of the help wanted section. Her eyes caught an item, and she picked up the phone and dialed the number listed. The phone rang four times before a woman with a hoarse voice answered. "Spencer's Model Agency and Night Club. Gracie Spencer speaking."

Tanya paused a moment. "It's a model agency and night club."

"What can you do with those?" Jennifer said. "You'd better wait for other listings."

"I'm sorry," she said, about to hang up.

"Wait! Come to the Boulevard Palace," Gracie said. "I got the deal of the century."

"Her voice…so enchanting, like the Fairy Godmother in the

Cinderella's movie," Tanya whispered to Jennifer. "Let's check this place."

Jennifer and Tanya hailed a cab. When they got to the palace, an elderly woman, who looked all of fifty-seven, thin, gray hair, an oval face and brown eyes, met them at the door.

"Come in." She squinted at the outside light, grabbed their hands and pulled them inside.

Tanya and Jennifer found themselves standing in a dimly lit room decorated in silver and blue with a large dance floor surrounded by silver cocktail tables and blue chairs. "What a lot of silver and blue crystal balls," Tanya observed, gazing at the ceiling. "The size of grapefruit, and surrounded by a huge, glass ball, hanging from the ceiling over the dance floor?"

"The room has no windows. The satin sashes extending from the walls, where windows would have been installed, makes the place appear larger," Gracie offered, and gazed at Tanya. "How old are you, my dear?"

"Twenty-one, Ma'am."

"Please! I'm not ancient," she sounded insulted. "Call me, Gracie. Have you ever done any modeling?"

"No, only dancing."

Gracie thought for a moment, hesitated, then said, "I need a partner for this place and that takes money."

"I got money. What's your price?"

"Forty thousand a month keeps this place running. I owe twice that on the mortgage."

"I'm searching for something that'll make money," Tanya said. "The business could pay off in the future and make me independent for life. What you think, Jennifer?"

"In the long run, it could be a good investment. When I finish my designing class, we can do well.

"I'll take a chance," Tanya said.

Gracie threw her hands up, grabbed Jennifer and gave her a big hug. "Come to my office. Lets draw up a contract. We'll go over the business routine tomorrow."

"Don't you wan 'a know all about me?" Tanya asked.

Gracie shook her head. "No. I like what I see."

After signing the contract, Tanya and Jennifer went back to the Hilton, had dinner, explored what the hotel had to offer then, went back to the room to go to bed.

The next day, at noon, They returned to the palace. Gracie showed them around and discussed the business. Several days later, after getting settled in the business, Tanya and Jennifer were having lunch at the Golden Apple Restaurant on Sunset Boulevard. They sat, casually looking around at the people entering and leaving the restaurant, when Jennifer noticed a man sitting one table over. He stared at her without blinking.

Could this be someone Joe had hired to find her? She sat there hoping he'd leave and when he didn't, she became paranoid. "I'll finish my coffee." She nervously gulped the last drop and ran from the restaurant, pulling Tanya's sleeve and glancing back to see if he had followed.

A week later, when she visited the club, the man that she thought Joe had sent, sat in one of the booths. He nodded and she reluctantly did the same.

"Nice club," he said. "I like the atmosphere."

"My sister would be pleased," she said, gazing at him.

"If it's not too presumptuous of me, would you join me for a drink?"

"Sorry. I haven't finished my homework," she said and walked away.

He called after her, "what about later, Miss…?"

"Greene." She rolled her eyes in disbelief. Why did she tell him her name?

"May I return later?"

"I'm never without homework here, but I take a break at ten o'clock." She'd learn what that snoop wants.

"My name's Steven Rollins. I'll be back," he said, got up and left.

Jennifer watched him leave. He's tall, dark and powerfully built, a man of twenty-five, or older. She remembered his deep set, hazel brown eyes, which had a lonely, but gentle warm glow when he smiled at her. Enough of this foolishness. She shook her head to get him out of her mind.

When she saw Steven, enter the club, the clock behind the bar struck ten. "Would you like a drink?" she asked, as casually as she could manage, when he sat on the stool in front of her.

"Johnnie Walker Black," he answered, and gave her body a raking gaze.

Jennifer noticed as he watched her. She poured his drink and a glass of champagne for herself. "Let's take a table." She motioned for the bartender to carry their drinks. They sat at a table for two near the corner in the back of the club.

Steven talked about himself, "I don't get out often at night. I have an invalid sister. She's time consuming."

"Long illness?" Jennifer asked, still suspicious of him. He's disturbing in every way.

"Three years," he answered, and slowly dropped his gaze from her face to her breast. "She's got a weak heart."

Jennifer kept her eyes trained on him. "How can you work and care for her?"

"I'm a builder by day. A nursemaid by night," he said and laughed, then looked seriously at her. "No joke. I hired a day nurse."

"Why are you out tonight?" She asked, not believing him.

"She's in the hospital for test."

They sat and talked till closing time, and Steven didn't want to leave her. "May I drive you home?"

"I've my own car," she answered. He wanted to know my address to report to Joe.

He stood as she arose, and he looked longingly at her. "May I see you again?"

She looked at him for a long moment, hesitated, then said, "Meet me at the Golden Apple for lunch tomorrow." She was by no means blind to his attraction, and something in his manner fascinated her.

"I haven't enjoyed the company of a woman in three years. I'll be there."

"I haven't had as much fun with anybody as I've had with you tonight," she said.

"Come on! A beauty like you must've had many dates."

"It's a long story. Can't go into it now."

He held her hand. "I'd like to know everything about you. But I can wait. Let's have another drink."

"I can't. It's one o'clock already. I've got to get back to studying. We can have dinner tomorrow night."

"Where?" he asked, looking pleased.

"My house." She wrote the address on a piece of paper and handed it to him. If he were someone Joe had hired, now was the time to expose him.

The following evening, Jennifer left school and went home early. She let the cook off and began preparing dinner for Steven and herself. "It has to be a delicious dinner," she muttered, doing the recipe for game hens that Gracie had given her. When she'd put the hens in the oven, she prepared French onion soup as an appetizer, carrots, watercress sushi, a green salad and angel food cake with strawberry sauce. It was eight o'clock when Steven rang her doorbell. She opened the door and he stood there with flowers before his face.

"Guess who?"

"Steven!" She exclaimed and took the flowers.

He had combed his fluffy black hair to the left, in a swirl type hairdo, and his sideburns were neatly brushed. She gazed at him, smiled and smelled the flowers. "How did you know that I liked red roses?"

"Someone so beautiful had to love colorful flowers."

A pink blush stung her cheeks. "C'mon in. Pour yourself a drink while I put these in water."

After dinner, they had drinks in the den.

Steven expressed appreciation for her cooking, "I haven't eaten a delicious home-cooked meal since my Mom died."

"When?"

"Gladys, my sister, was ten, and I was thirteen."

"Any other relatives?"

"Not now. Mom's sister came and took care of us. She died after I'd finished architectural school," his voice dropped in volume, and a look of sadness came into his eyes. "Just me and Gladys now."

"You're blessed to have finished with a career," she said, and told him about her dream of going to college. They talked till two in the morning.

"I must get home. The nurse is competent, but Gladys demands a talk, before she goes to sleep."

They said goodnight with a handshake. Though she longed for him to take her in his arms, she thought it best not to spoil it till they know each other better, and for fear that he'd get the wrong impression.

The next day, Jennifer got to the club early. Many calls came in for bookings.

"We need a secretary," Gracie said, answering three phones at a time.

Tanya agreed, "I'll place an ad in the paper."

By six o'clock, Jennifer was about to leave the club when Steven telephoned, "may I come over tonight?"

"I'm on my way home," she said. "Meet me there."

When Jennifer drove up, Steven was parked outside her house. She opened the door to her living room and he followed her inside. "I longed to spend the evening with you," he said. His gaze riveted on her face, then traveled slowly over her body.

Her heart jolted and her pulse pounded, as she blushed and looked away. "It's a warm night. How about a swim?"

They went outside to the dressing room near the pool. Jennifer changed into a two piece, powder blue, bikini set. She dove into the pool and came to the surface as Steven removed his pants and shirt. He dove into the pool in his boxer shorts, and Jennifer laughed when she saw his shorts stuck to his skin.

"Laughed at me, huh?" He pulled her back in the water, drew her close, and kissed her a long moment, before they surfaced.

The touch of his lip on hers sent a shock wave throughout her body. She felt a burning desire, and an aching need for another kiss. "I've never tasted kisses like yours."

"Haven't you ever been in love?"

"No, and I never dreamed anyone would love me, "she said.

"You've got to be kidding. Boys must've noticed you."

"When most girls dated, I worked."

They got out of the pool and sat on the patio in the loungers. Steven's shorts, made of thin cotton, revealed his dark, smooth muscles. She found herself extremely conscious of his virile appeal, and her heart raced when their eyes met.

He took her in his arms. "I'm wild about you," he said, showering kisses around her lips, along her jaw, in the hollow of her neck, then her eyes, and, finally, he satisfyingly kissed her soft mouth.

Her heart thumped wildly, and she bit her lip. "I'm falling in love with you, but I've no right."

A shadow of alarm touched his face. "What do you mean?"

Her breath caught in her throat. She looked up into his eyes and confessed, "I'm married."

His dark eyes showed the tortured dullness of disbelief, and he blinked in bewilderment as he let go of her and sat up. "Where's your husband?"

She told him her life's story, including how she had been tricked into marriage.

He drew her to him in a renewed embrace. "My poor darling." He planted kisses on her lips between each word, "you…didn't…deserve that." They lay in each other arms till midnight. Finally, he said, "I got to get home to Gladys."

After Steven left, Jennifer went to bed, but she couldn't sleep. She thought of Joe. How could she could ask for a divorce without revealing her location. When she fell asleep, it was past three a.m., and ten a.m. when she awoke.

Gracie was peeved with her when she arrived at the club. "You promised to help us. Though it's Saturday, it would've helped a lot if you'd gotten here on time."

"Had a problem gnawing at my gut," Jennifer answered, "Couldn't sleep."

Gracie came back at her, "Ain't nobody around here without problems."

"Ok. I'm sorry. It won't happen again."

"Don't mean to be hard. But I can't trust others handling the money. Almost lost this place once. Tanya and I can't afford to make the same mistake."

"Take off. Get some sleep. I'll handle everything."

Later that night, Jennifer was busy booking models when Steven entered the club. He headed straight for her, took her in his arms and held her close. You look lovely, beautifully put together as last evening," he said, holding her. "What a spectacular body." A sense of urgency overtook him as he held her. "I ached for your touch. Can we do something tonight?"

"Can't. I promised to stay late," she said, longingly at him. "I Won't be home till two."

"I've got to be with you. May I come later?"

A tingling in the pit of her stomach made her hand him the key to her house. "I'll be home when I can get out of here."

Jennifer got home two-thirty in the morning and found Steven waiting. He poured a glass of wine and handed it to her as she sat on the sofa. "I got here at midnight. I wanted to see you when you came though the door."

"You're a kind, thoughtful man." She took his face in both hands and kissed his lips. "I don't think I've ever worked so hard as I did today."

"I should be here for you all the time," he said. "Marry me."

A soft gasp escaped her, as she looked at him in surprise. "I've thought about a divorce, but what about Gladys?"

"The Doctor has given her a few months, but she's holding on. I've got to think of something," he said, holding her. "I want to lay beside you at night and wake up next to you every morning."

"Me too, Steven," she admitted. "But we can't do anything to hurt Gladys."

"I'm telling her tomorrow. She's got to understand. I need a life of my own."

Jennifer swam through a haze of feelings and desires. Part of her wanted him to tell Gladys, and part of her couldn't live with the consequences. "Don't tell her yet. Wait till I contact Joe." A flicker of apprehension coursed through her and she said a silent prayer. Lord, let Joe be reasonable. Could she, in all these months, contact Joe? The idea of letting him know where she was, frightened her. He wasn't a person that easily accepted rejection. He always took what he'd wanted and gotten it. Power excited him.

Steven, happy with the idea of contacting Joe, broadened his smile in approval. "Let's drink to our coming freedom." He poured a glass of wine and lifted his glass in a solute, "To us, forever, sweetheart."

The idea sent her spirits soaring and her heart danced with excitement. "I love being in your arms."

He drew her closer, then let go abruptly. "This is unbearable. I've got to go home now or I won't be able to leave."

"Until tomorrow night," she said and kissed him goodbye.

Jennifer placed a call to Kentucky. Joe answered the phone.

"Where are you, darling? Why you leave me?"

"You know the answer," she said, coldly. "I couldn't stay as your wife. I don't love you."

"Don't say what you don't mean," he said, sounding dejected.

"Our life was unreal," she said, hoping to get him to agree. "There's a big difference in our ages."

Chapter 6

"Tell me where you are," he pleaded, ignoring what she had said. "California," she answered, hesitantly. "We need to talk." "Sure, darling. I'll come and bring you home." Her words were cool and clear as ice water. "You don't get it. I want a divorce."

When he spoke again, his voice was tender, almost a murmur. "You're upset. You don't know what you're saying. What's your address?"

"Promise me you'll talk and not try to change my mind."

"Sure, darling," he promised, knowing that he had no intentions of keeping his word.

After talking with Joe, Jennifer sat quietly, for a moment, and prayed. Dear Lord, I...I don't know if I'm doing the right thing, contacting Joe. Please help me. All I know is, I can't go on like this. I want to be free to marry the man that I love.

A week passed, since Jennifer had spoken with Joe, then two, and one evening, while Tanya made her usual rounds, she came to one of the tables, turned around and stared into Joe's face. She remembered him from the picture Jennifer had shown her, and she rushed to the table where Jennifer sat.

Joe suspiciously followed Tanya. "Well look-ee here," he said, nonchalantly. "So, this is what you've come to, drinking in a whore house with this club as a front."

She jolted, gasped and angrily, rolled her eyes at him. "What do you mean?"

He gazed at her with a bland half smile. "I could drop fifty cents to the tabloids about this place."

"My sister and her partner run a respectable business." She, clenched her jaw and narrowed her eyes. "They wouldn't believe you."

His shaggy, thick brows lifted upward. "People like to think the worse. They'll hear what I have to tell 'em, and they'll close this place tomorrow."

"Respectable people use our services," Tanya stated. "They'd know you're lying."

He laughed, shook his head and said, "you naive strumpet, eighty-five percent don't use this place; the rest would swear they never heard of you."

Jennifer looked at him with hatred in her eyes. He was threatening her, and forcing her to make a choice that would put her back in hell. But at the moment, if she, Tanya and Gracie were disgraced, she'd still be in hell. She wished she hadn't contacted him and she was desperate to come up with some way to stop him. "If I can prove you defrauded me, lied to me and tricked me into marriage, you think anybody would believe you?"

"I'm a husband, trying to separate his wife from a worn out old prostitute and a stripper. They'd believe me."

"You can't say that about Gracie and Tanya. Get out!" She pushed him toward the door.

Joe rushed toward her and held her wrist. "Do you believe I'm so stupid as to let you steal my hard earned cash, lie to me and have the nerve to think I'd let you leave me?"

"What I took was mine." She squirmed to get free. "I earned the money."

"You're coming with me, now."

Steven entered the club. When he saw Joe with his hands on Jennifer, he charged him like a bull and knocked him to the floor.

Joe got up and swore at him, "You lowlife. I'll have you jailed for this. Who the hell are you? One of her tricks?"

Steven started for him again, and Jennifer stopped him, "let it go. He's not worth the trouble."

Joe hurried out, shook his fist at Steven, and shouted obscenities.

"Who was that clown?" asked Steven with his fist balled.

"My husband, and he's trouble."

"He'll get trouble," declared Steven, his arms around her. "He won't bother you while I'm around."

"I'm seeing a lawyer tomorrow, "she said, her eyebrows slanting in a worried frown. "I don't trust Joe."

That next day, Jennifer was about to leave for her appointment with her lawyer when she got a call.

"Ms. Morgan? Dr. Bonner, here. Your husband was brought to St. Joseph's, shot in both knees."

Jennifer rushed to St. Joseph's Hospital. The doctor met her at the admittance desk.

"Your husband is stabilized. He's a diabetic. Lost both knees and had to have replacements."

"No!" she cried. "This can't happen."

"I'm sorry. He'll need therapy wherever he's transferred, but he'll learn to walk again."

She went inside Joe's room. He looked at her and beckoned, "come closer." Unspoken pain was alive and glowing in his eyes, and he spoke with a possessive desperation, "I played poker with guests in the hotel where I stayed. One bastard cheated, I hit him, and he shot me. I'm goin 'a need you now, Jenni. You gotta' come home with me."

She backed away. "I can't."

His voice hardened ruthlessly. "I meant what I said about the tabloids. You, your sister, and that whore will walk the streets."

She swallowed hard, lifted her chin and boldly met his eyes. "I wasn't on the street when I met you, and neither Tanya, nor Gracie. We can take care of ourselves."

His angry gaze swung over her. "You can, maybe, but Gracie's too old to start over. Is that what you want for your friend?"

She shot him a cold look and hurried out of the room. Nauseating despair sank inside her gut. What would she tell Gracie and Tanya? It was all over for them?

When Gracie heard the news, she cried, "If you leave him, what am I to do? I can't make it alone. Yet, I can't ask you to sacrifice your life for me."

"I'll be here," Tanya tried to assure her. "I can keep this place running."

Gracie ignored Tanya, put her arms around Jennifer and pleaded with her, "Can't you persuade him without returning to Kentucky? You don't owe him anything."

Dismay lodged in her stomach. "I'm still married to him." Tears filled her eyes.

"He'll make trouble for us."

"Can't you put him in a nursing home?" Tanya asked, and pressed her hands over her face. You've gained too much to go back to nothing. Say he lost his mind."

"I can't. I see no other way out than to go back." Then she thought about Steven. "I got to let Steven know." She went to the phone and dialed his number.

Steven heard the despair in her voice. "What's wrong?"

"Joe got hurt. He can't walk. I'm going back with him." She started crying.

"No, Jennifer, wait. We'll work something out."

"Nothing can be done. I'm trapped. Bye, Steven." She put the receiver in its holder before he could respond, and she ran out to her car. The drive home was blurry. When she got home, she threw clothes in several suitcases, not bothering folding anything, tossed the luggage in the trunk of the car, then drove to the hospital.

Joe sat in his wheelchair, ready to be taken to the airport for the trip home. When he saw Jennifer, his face lit with a bright smile. "I knew you'd come to your senses and realize we belong together."

Her throat ached with defiance. "Returning to the ranch is temporary. Till you're better and able to handle things yourself, "she sputtered, bristling with indignation. "When you're well, I want a divorce."

74

"That's a joke." He laughed in a weird sort of way. "Better? Face it. I'm a cripple for life." Then he yelled obscenities at her, and Jennifer ran out of the room with both hands to her ears.

She knew what he had said was true. He'd never walk again, even with the replacements. He'd use it as an excuse to hang onto her.

Joe continued yelling, "A cripple, do you hear?" He laughed and yelled like a mad man until, Morley came and put him in the car.

The next day, after arriving in Kentucky, Jennifer hired a male nurse to take care of Joe, and she kept to herself in her bedroom. He didn't like that arrangement, "A wife's suppose to sleep with her husband."

"In this house, we're not man and wife," she replied in a low tormented voice. "I'm the hired help."

"You're a whore. A cheap slut." He wanted to hurt her. "Your people are poor trash. Don't you know I had 'em checked out?"

His voice, cold and lashing, tore at her soul. She faced him, her heart paining. A swift shadow of anger swept across her face. Furious, she could hardly speak, "Yes, my people are poor, but we never asked for handouts. All of us worked hard for what we got."

He relished the words, and the wounds he inflicted upon her, "you lived in a bad, rundown, neighborhood. You didn't have a pot to pee in. This should be heaven for you here."

Once upon a time, I thought it would," she reminisced. "Living with family, those you love, is more important than material things."

His voice restrained, yet held an undertone of cold contempt, "You have no college degree," he chuckled, nastily. "You couldn't earn enough for this kinda life, if you had one."

"I had the chance for a degree," she said, tears rolling down her cheeks. "You stole that away."

"I've saved you a lot of heartache and worry. Why study a bunch of books hoping to get what you already have?"

"It would mean more with an education," she tried to say, but he wouldn't listen.

He laughed. "Wise up, girl, other women would kill to have what you've got."

Was he crazy? She turned a vivid scarlet and lashed out at him, "what exactly have you given that's so great? You ruined my first chance of an education, stole my virginity...and, now, a second time...I should be grateful?"

"You bet. You're not the scholar you'd like to think you are. What can you do besides cook and clean?" He wheeled his chair in front of her. "You had a lot of hopes and dreams that had no chance of coming true."

The way he said it made her sad. Alarm and anger rippled through her spine, and more tears flooded her eyes. "You don't know me or what I can do."

He whirled his wheelchair closer. Quick anger rose in his eyes. "I know you, and all women like you. You believe you should have equal rights; you want to do all the things men do."

Fury almost chocked her, but she yelled at him, "Who died and made you King of the jungle? Male chauvinist pig." She hurried to her room and slammed the door shut.

He angrily wheeled himself to his room, took a gun out of the dresser drawer, cradled it in his bosom, then hid it in bed under his pillar.

Jennifer didn't come to dinner, and Joe stayed in his room, all week, where he took his meals and listened to country music.

***

Three months passed. Jennifer was lonely and yearned for California. Bill had written and asked to come to stay with her. Maybe, he could help to ease her pain and suffering. That evening, instead of staying in her room, she joined Joe for dinner.

"My brother is in need of a job," she said, with an anxious look on her face. "It would be wonderful to have one of my family here."

Joe gave her a big smile. "Your family is my family. Bill would be welcomed here."

A warm glow flowed through her cheeks and the tension between her and Joe began to melt.

They were civil to one another all week.

Bill arrived the following week. Jennifer waited at the airport for him. When his plane landed, she ran to him, and they embraced for a long moment.

"Thanks for the plane fare," he said, and kissed her. "Mamma sends her love. Pop didn't say nothing. He got money, after they found asbestos on the ship where he worked. Mamma quit her job and hired some help. Pop's the same."

Bill referred to Mr. Jack, as Pop; probably, a male identity thing. She and Tanya never accepted him as their dad.

On the way to the ranch, Jennifer told Bill about her dilemma, and he swore to look out for her.

When they arrived at the ranch, Joe welcomed Bill, "my house is yours. Morley will get anything you need. I'll put you on the payroll and in charge of transporting horses from people who need studs."

Months rolled by, and Bill made life a little easier for her. She spent most of her time with him. One day, she had to go to town to shop. Afterwards, she stopped in at the Ramada Inn for lunch. She was enjoying a Turkey club sandwich, when Steven sat at her table. "Steven!" She rushed into his arms. "I've missed you."

They clung together for a few seconds, then he looked at her, with sadness in his eyes. "Gladys died, and it's been hell without you."

"I'm sorry. Must've been awful for you."

"I'm free to marry now," he said, holding her, wrapping his arms around her like a warm blanket. He stroked her hair softly.

She stared into his eyes, longing for him. "Oh, Steven, don't make it hard for me." She swallowed the sob that arose in her throat.

"Listen to me, Jennifer, he can't hold you. You've done all you can."

"It's been hell for me, too," she said, hot tears rolling down her cheeks. "He's become a drunk. He yells at me, treats me like dirt and accuses me of having sex with his ranch hands."

"You can't stay there any longer. I'm taking you away, but first, I'm going to deal with him."

A new anguish seared her heart. "No! I'm afraid. If you confronted Joe…I'll have to do it alone. You mustn't ever come to the ranch."

Jennifer left Steven and went back to the ranch. When she got in the house, she hurried to Joe's room. He sat in his wheelchair, reading a book. When he saw her, he smiled and put the book aside. "Darling, have you come to tell me you're coming back to my bed?"

His words annoyed her. How could he have the audacity to think that she would ever sleep with him again? "No. I've been here a year and six months, and all we do is argue. Neither of us is happy."

His face turned hateful. "You wanna' run out again, huh? Well forget it. It ain't going 'a happen. You'll stay till one of us dies." He wheeled himself over to her, took her wrist, and twisted her arm.

"You're hurting me," she cried, straining back against his arm and twisting free.

"That's not all I'll do if you try 'an leave."

She saw his eyes. Large glittering ovals, with a burning, far away look. "You're mad. You've given up on life, and you want to take me with you."

He let go of her and pleaded, "What am I suppose to do? A cripple with no family, and nobody to care for me."

"You got Morley."

"He ain't kin. I need you, Jenni. Please, don't leave me." He held her about the waist as she turned her back to him, holding her so tightly that she lost her balance and fell into his lap. "Let go of me, Joe." She struggled free, and her brown eyes blazed. She faced him furiously. "I'll stay, but you got to stop drinking and learn to walk."

He wrapped his arms around her midriff. "Thank you darling. I'm gonna' do what you want."

She pushed him away, left and went to her room. "Dammit!" She kicked the corner of her bed. Why did she let him get to her? She flung herself on the bed. Deep sobs racked her insides. He always managed to change her mind. I won't be stuck with him. "I won't!" She yelled, got up and sat by her window. Depleted and motionless, she tried to reserve her strength. If she gave up now, he would win, and she would be powerless.

Later, that evening, she didn't have dinner with Joe or Bill, but got dressed and went to the driveway. As she was leaving, Morley brought the car around. "I don't need you," she said. "I'll drive."

"Yes, Ms. Jennifer." He got out of the car and handed the keys to her. Joe wheeled himself to the window and watched her get into the car. He buzzed for Morley.

"Yes sir," Morley answered.

"Follow her. Keep me informed of her activities."

"Sir?" he asked with his mouth open.

"Are you deaf?" he yelled. "I wanna' know where she goes."

"Yes sir," Morley said, backing out of the room with a nervous look on his face. He got the silver Lincoln and sped out of the drive, leaving a cloud of white dust from the loose gravel that covered the drive. When he caught up with Jennifer, he stayed a distance of five cars behind her.

Jennifer parked in front of the Marriott's Griffin Gate Resort, gave her keys to the valet, and went into the Pegasus Restaurant. She sat at a table for two and ordered from the menu. While waiting to be served, she ordered champagne and watched people entering and leaving the restaurant. She took a cigarette from her golden cigarette case, placed one in her mouth and fished in her purse for her lighter. A flame flickered from a golden lighter, and lit her cigarette.

Jennifer looked up into the eyes of Steven. "I wanted to call you," she said, as he sat beside her. "I didn't have the heart." Her anguish almost over came her control. She took a sip of champagne, swallowed hard, then took a deep breath and tried to relax.

"You told him?"

She cleared her throat, and squeezed her eyes shut, trying to hold back tears. "I wanted to kill him. For the first time in my life, I wanted to shoot the man in his wheelchair, and leave him there. It's hopeless."

"Don't say that. You're stronger than he. What happened?"

"He begged me not to leave. If only you could've seen him. He was pathetic," she said, drew heavily on her cigarette and blew it to the ceiling.

Steven grew furious. "You can't let him get away with that," he said through clenched teeth. "He's using your good nature and kindness to manipulate you."

"I know, but what can I do?" she replied, her mind languid, without hope.

His lips thinned with more anger, and he suggested, "Give him an ultimatum."

"I told him I'd stay till he'd stopped drinking, and learned to walk again."

"Aw, Jennifer, that could take forever!" He held her chin and gazed into her eyes. "He'll always make excuses." He kissed her lips. "I love you and I want to marry you. You've been with that jerk long enough."

She sank into his arms, swimming through a haze of feelings and desires, wanting to escape with him, and to leave everything behind. She was sick with the struggle within her. What had happened to the level-headed young woman of yesterday? No, she had to stay and confront her responsibilities. "I'll have Morley remove every bottle of liquor from the house. He'll have to dry out then."

"Enough about him," he said. "Let's talk about us. I'm staying here till this thing is resolved."

A warm glow of strength flow through her, and she kissed him. "It's comforting knowing you're near."

He kissed her lips softly. "I'm not leaving till we go together. No matter how long it takes, we're going to be married." They sat there and talked until the restaurant closed.

"It's late. I've got to go," she said, and swallowed the despair in her throat.

He took her hand and walked her outside. "Will I see you tomorrow?"

"I'll come, Saturday." She kissed him and waited for her car.

The parking attendant brought her car, and Steven helped her inside. He leaned his head in the window and kissed her goodbye. When she arrived home, she noticed the lights were on in Joe's room. He sat listening to his favorite bluegrass record and singing loudly to the beat of the music. She tipped lightly by his door till she got in her room.

Chapter 7

That morning, after breakfast, Jennifer called Morley to the den. "I'm going to need your help to get Joe to quit drinking. Remove all the liquor and replace it with soda, coffee, tea or anything non-alcoholic."

"Yes, Ms. Jennifer, but it shore's gon' be a shock to him when he finds it gone." He rubbed his bearded face and pulled his mustache.

"He and I made a pact. He agreed. It'll be all right."

"Yes, Ms. Jennifer, you're the boss." He gave her a wink and a wide smile, showing tobacco stained teeth.

Morley removed all of the whiskey from the bar, the kitchen and the den. That included everything under Joe's bed, where he kept a case of bourbon hidden.

Later that evening, all hell broke loose. Joe bellowed for Morley. "Where's my damn box? Who's been in my room? I've been robbed."

Jennifer and Morley ran to Joe's room. "What's all the fuss?" She asked, her expression grim as she watched him.

"Somebody stole my case," he yelled, waved his arms, and rolled his wheelchair around.

"Calm down, Joe. I had Morley rid you of all your temptations."

The corners of his mouth twisted with exasperation. "Dammit it, woman. Why didn't you leave that up to me?"

"You promised to quit drinking. If your intentions were real, why are you upset?"

"I was gonna do it myself." He slammed his chair into his bed, his broad shoulders heaved as he breathed. "You got my ranch hands guffawing and snickering behind my back."

Jennifer's eyes firmed, her tone hardened. "And when were you going to get around to it, Joe? Next month? Next year?"

"A half glass a day. I can't do cold turkey, woman."

"You can now," she said, and gazed at him through narrowed eyes.

His annoyance increased when he looked at her face. Now, she was the victim of his brutal stare. "You've ruined my reputation, and you've robbed me of the chance to regain my respect and my manhood."

"I'm helping you," she countered icily, and left the room.

After lunch, Joe wheeled himself to the table. He waited for Jennifer to join him, and called to her as she passed the dining room, "You gonna' join me?"

"Got an appointment in town," she said, glanced at herself in the mirror, and retouched her makeup. "I'll get something while I'm out."

A faint threat of hysteria etched his voice. "What about dinner?"

"Won't be back in time. Go 'head without me." She left, got in her blue Lincoln, and drove away.

Joe rang for Morley. "Follow her. Let me know if she sees that same looser."

Morley drove out behind her and caught up with her. He parked and watched her go inside the Hyatt. This time, she didn't stay late, and arrived back home at eleven o'clock. Shortly after, she went to bed, Morley came home and reported to Joe.

Joe slammed the arms of his wheelchair with both fists. "I 'mo teach that bastard a lesson. Get some men together. Pay 'em two hundred a piece."

"Yes sir." He smiled and tipped his large cowboy's hat. "I know a few who'd be right for the job."

"Do it, tonight!" he said, his voice hard, cold and evil.

Morley took the blue Ford pickup truck and went back to town.

He returned later, around two that morning, and quietly knocked on Joe's door. "It's done, sir."

"Y 'all a' get a bonus for this,' Joe said, laughed loudly and went back to sleep.

Seven o'clock that morning, before Jennifer got out of bed, her phone rang. She rolled over and answered.

"Jennifer?" Steven whispered in a low, painful tone.

She sprang up in bed. "Steven! What's wrong?"

"Some men broke into my room. They beat me."

"I'm on my way." She jumped out of bed, grabbed a dress from the closet, and hurried to her car. Her foot pushed the accelerator to the floor, and the wheels screeched and hollowed till she arrived at the Hyatt. She ran inside, not bothering parking the car, stepped on the elevator and kept her finger on the button till she reached the third floor. When the elevator stopped, the doors barely opened when she pushed her way out, ran down the hall to Steven's room and banged on his door.

Steven opened the door and she rushed into his arms. "Oh! Your face. Who did this to you?"

"Twelve-thirty, I answered the door. Four men threw me to the floor, beat and kicked me.

One said, as they left, 'that'll teach you to leave our women alone."

Jennifer cast a flabbergasted expression. "You know any women here?"

"None, other than you," he answered, through swollen lips.

Jennifer paced the floor. Then it hit her hard. "He wouldn't...I don't...believe..."

"What?" He rose to his feet holding his jaw.

"Joe could've hired someone. No! That's crazy."

"He doesn't know I'm here," Steven said.

"Unless..." She stopped pacing, and sat beside him. "I'm going to get to the bottom of this. I got to go back to the ranch."

"I'm coming with you." He went to his closet and removed his pants and shirt.

"No, you mustn't get involved."

"I'm already involved." He got into his clothes.

"Please, let me handle this alone." Jennifer left Steven and drove home as fast as she had driven to town. It was time to put her cards on the table. She parked in the drive and went straight to Joe's room. He sat in his wheelchair with a drink in his hand.

"You miserable liar," she yelled the words in his face. "You never intended to keep your word."

"I tried," he said, rolled toward her and held her hands. "You don't know what it's like being in this chair, a strapping, hardy man like me who's use to riding and roping horses." He leaned back in his chair and the light from his lamp revealed the deepened lines of despair on his face.

A strange look in his eyes made her shudder, but she continued to blast him, "It was your own doing."

"What do you mean?"

"Your doctor told you to practice walking, and your damnable, fiery temper made everyone around you miserable. You had somebody beat Steven, didn't you?"

He wasn't about to confess his deed. "I don't have a clue what you're talking about."

"Don't lie to me," she said, staring him in the eye. "Nobody here knows Steven."

"Ok! What if I did? Coming here, parading behind my back, and for all my friends to see."

Jennifer got angry and sputtered with outrage, "I should 'a known I couldn't trust you. I'm through talking." She turned to leave.

Joe wheeled himself in her path. "I'm sorry. I'll get rid of the whiskey. Please don't say you leaving."

She moved away. "It ain't in you to keep your word. Anyway, I've been here long enough. I've done more than my duty. It's time I left." She hurried to her room to pack.

Joe removed the gun from his pillar and wheeled himself in her room. "I tried to give you a life. A real life with kids and all the money you'd ever need."

"Don't you see? I'm a city girl. I need neon lights, academy awards, music and theaters. It can never work between us."

"It could if you let it."

"Face it, Joe, I don't want you." She continued packing. "This would be unhappiness and an earthly death for me. Some things are just not meant to be."

"You ain't going nowhere," he yelled, his face a glowing mask of rage. "I'll kill you before I let you leave me."

"You're crazy!" she exclaimed, looking at him with terror in her eyes, trying not to appear frightened. "Get out of my way."

"No! Get in my room." He stuck the gun to her back, pushed her, and wheeled himself behind her. "All I ever wanted was for you to love me. I'd do anything for you." He got her in his room, and kissed her hand, as he held her arm. "Why couldn't you love me?"

"It's no use talking about this," she said, shuddering with fear. "I'll never love you."

"Well, bitch, If I can't have you, nobody will." He pulled the trigger.

The gun didn't fire, and Jennifer screamed.

Bill heard her and came to the window. "Joe, what're you doing? Put the gun down."

"Get away from my window. Mind your own damn business."

"Hold on, Sis. I'm coming."

Jennifer stood motionless as she trembled in fear for her life, while Joe pushed the button on his chair with one hand and pointed the gun at her with the other. "I'm mo' kill you, bitch."

Then, she got angry. A wave of genuine, physical strength swamped her. "You can't hold me here. Go 'head, shoot!"

"You'd rather die than stay with me? Well, I can oblige you." He pulled the trigger again.

A terrifying sound pierced Jennifer's ears. K-Pow, K-Pow. Bullets whined over her head. Her body trembled. She was sure that she was going to die. K-Pow. Then she thought, either he didn't want to kill her or he was a bad shot, but she wasn't going to wait and find out.

She ran out of the room as fast as her legs would let her move. A few minutes lapsed then she heard another shot, K-pow. She screamed and ran back inside. Bill followed. Her eyes fell on Joe's head, as blood oozed from his forehead.

Bill rushed into the room. "Call an ambulance," he shouted, and ran outside.

Jennifer stumbled out to the hall and sat in the arm chair by Joe's room, her thin fingers, numbed, tensed in her lap. After what seemed like hours, but only thirty minutes, she heard police siren's blaring, then someone banging on the door. "Open the door Bill. I don't have the strength to move."

Bill opened the door. The police and an ambulance descended upon Joe's bedroom. After searching his room, the questions began: "I'm Sargent Taylor. What happened here?"

She blinked and stared blindly into Sargent Taylor's face, as she relived that last horrible moment. "My husband and I argued. He pulled a gun and threatened to kill me." She shook, clutched her chest with both hands and sobbed.

Sargent Taylor commanded his officers, "Get her some water."

One of his officers returned and handed her the glass, and Sargent Taylor waited for her to finish.

Jennifer took long sips then, began, "Joe pulled the trigger, and the gun jammed twice before firing. I ran from the room. Then I heard a shot. My brother and I came in and found him."

Sargent Taylor turned to Bill. "Are you her brother?"

"Yes Sargent," he answered. His voice drifted into a hushed whisper.

"Did you see what happened?" he asked, eyeing his suspiciously.

"I looked through this window, after she screamed. Joe had this gun on her." He lifted the gun up with a pencil and handed it to him.

"Yeah? But he's the one shot!" Sargent Taylor replied with heavy irony.

"I don't know what happened," she said, irritated by his critical tone. "I guess he shot himself."

Sargent Taylor gazed at Jennifer for a long moment, then said,

"There's going to be an inquest. I'll need both of you down at headquarters."

The paramedics put Joe's body in the ambulance and left. Sargent Taylor and his men followed.

Later that night, Jennifer tried to sleep. She screamed and sat up in bed.

Bill rushed into her room. "It's all right, Sis. You're dreaming."

"I went through the whole ordeal again," she said and held onto him.

He cradled her. "You'll make it, Sis."

Jennifer thought about Steven, let go of Bill and dialed his number. Steven's phone rang several times before she gave up, and after putting the phone back on it's receiver, she heard the doorbell ring and opened it to find him standing on her doorstep.

He rushed inside and took her in his arms. "Are you all right, darling? I heard everything on the news."

"It was horrible." She clung to him, crying on his shoulder. "He lost his mind."

"Don't think about him. Come back to town with me."

"There's liable to be talk," she warned him. "I don't want 'em saying bad things about you."

"I don't care. Let them talk, " he said. "I'm concerned for you. We can send for your things later."

"I don't want nothing associated with this place. I came here with nothing and I'll leave that way."

Bill entered the hall. She introduced him to Steven.

"Take care my sister," he said, looking sadly at her.

"No need to worry. I love her and I'm going to marry her."

Jennifer hugged Bill. "This ranch is yours, she declared. "I 'm giving it to you with my blessing." She hugged him, took Steven's hand, and closed the door. Steven's helped her into the car and she didn't look back as he drove down the gravel drive to the main road.

At the inquest, Joe's death was ruled a homicide. "Your finger prints are on the gun," said Sargent Taylor. "You're under arrest. Anything you say can be held against you."

"No," Steven yelled. "You're wrong. She didn't shoot him."

Jennifer shook her head. Her brows drawn in an agonized expression. She whispered, "be quiet, Steven, they mustn't involve you."

Sargent Taylor turned and looked at Steven, then at Jennifer. "Is he your lover? Did you two plan this?"

Steven didn't answer. He rushed forward and hugged Jennifer."I'll post bail and get a lawyer."

She remained motionless in his arms for a moment. Then she pleaded, "Please, Steven, Don't get involved."

"I can't let you go alone," he said, still holding her.

The arresting officer rushed forward and roughly thrust Jennifer away from Steven, putting handcuffs on her.

Steven's mouth twisted in a threat, "Careful with her or you'll be sorry."

"Get along, said the officer, raising his night stick across Steven's stomach.

"Ok, enough of this," Sargent Taylor said. "If you're going to help her, don't get arrested."

Steven backed off and glared at the officer through resentful eyes. "Don't worry, sweet, I'll be back. He watched as Jennifer was led through the doors and held to be taken to the county detention center.

Jennifer didn't get any sleep. How could she, sitting in a corner on a cot with several women buzzing around, and gazing at her?

The next morning, Steven was at the jail with Lawyer Petrie. They paid her bail and she walked out with them. "Where are you staying?" Lawyer Petrie asked?"

"With me, at the Hyatt Regency Lexington," Steven answered.

"No, it would look better if she went back to the ranch."

"Better to whom?" Steven asked, with an anxious look on his face.

"If this case comes to trial, the prosecutor is going to make it look like she planned to killed him to be with you."

Steven jumped to him feet. "That's outrageous. She would never hurt anyone. Not even that loon."

"OK, you've got to stop with these outbursts," Petrie said. "You're making it look bad for her."

"I'm sorry. It's tearing me up inside to see her suffering because of that Madman." He held on to her hand not letting it go.

Petrie gazed at him, wondering about his involvement. "Where were you when he was shot?"

Jennifer slumped over with a worried expression. The question was a stab in her heart. "You think we planned Joe's murder?"

"No, but the jury will, after the prosecutor gets through with them." A nauseous sink of despair, and warning spasms of alarm erupted within her. She looked at Steven with an effort. "Please, leave me."

His expression was like someone struck in the face. "What? You're asking me to abandon you?"

"Until this is over. We'll find each other again."

Steven flung his hands in simple despair. "If this is what it's going to take to keep you from going to prison, I'll leave." He hugged her. "C'mon I'll drive you to the ranch."

When Steven saw her safely to the door, he kissed her for a long moment, and they stood there holding each other with tears in their eyes. "When this is over, we're going to be married," he declared. "No more waiting."

"I love you, Steven, and I want you, more than anything I've ever wanted."

Steven left and Jennifer went inside and straight to her room, passing joe's room with her eyes closed. She got in bed, closed her eyes, but couldn't sleep. Her heart ached with pain. God, how could she have come to this? All she ever wanted was to go to College and become somebody. Nothing turned out the way she planned.

The next morning was even harder than last night. She came out of her room only once to get a cup of tea. The cook glared at her with hatred in her eyes. Jennifer pierced her with an equal glare. "You got a problem?"

Tears filled her eyes. "Mr. Joe was always nice to me. Why did you kill him?"

"I didn't kill him, ok," she yelled. "Somebody else did." She flung the kettle in the sink, got her tea, stumbled out of the kitchen, and back to her bedroom. Her body shook as she cried angry, hot tears that scorched her cheeks. She lay in bed clinging to her soft satin pillow, and wished she'd never come to the ranch.

Around noon that day, Petrie call, "we're going to trial, unless you want to confess."

"No. I won't confess to something I didn't do."

"Ok, don't get upset. I just wanted to know."

"If you don't believe in my innocence, what's the point of defending me?" she ripped out the words impatiently.

"I wanted to make sure you believed it yourself," he insisted with returning impatience.

Chapter 8

The court room was packed with all the neighbors, people who knew Joe, and then some. The clerk called the court room to order, "All rise. Judge Jeremy Black residing."

Judge Black banged his gavel. "Be seated. Mr. Prosecutor, you may begin your questioning.

"Your Honor, I call Mr. Morley to the stand," said Prosecutor John Feldman.

Morley took the stand and was sworn in. "Mr. Morley, were Mr. and Mrs. Morgan a happy couple?"

"Objection, your honor, that's hear say."

"Objections sustained," said judge Black. "Rephrase the question."

"Mr. Morley, could you tell us what you observed in the Morgan household?"

"Well, sir, Mr. Joe and Ms. Jennifer had separate bedrooms."

Prosecutor Feldman faced the jury. "In other words, they didn't sleep together as man and wife?"

"No sir, not after the night he married 'er."

"Did they do anything together?"

"No, sir.

"Thank you, Mr. Morley."

"Mr. Petrie," Judge Black, motioned for him to question Morley.

"Mr. Morley, how did you know they didn't sleep together?"

"Mr. Joe married Ms. Jennifer after she had too much champagne." he said, grinning.

"He instructed me to drive to Judge Warp's house where he married 'er." Morley stared sheepishly at Jennifer.

A cold shiver spread over her as she remembered that night.

"Are you saying that she didn't marry him of her own free will?" Petrie asked.

"Yes sir," he said, nervously. "He held her up on her feet while Judge Warp performed the ceremony."

"What do you mean, held her up while he performed the ceremony?"

"Ms. Jennifer was drunk."

"Drunk?"

"Yes, sir, Mr. Joe gave her lots of champagne."

"No further questions," Petrie said. "I call Mrs. Morgan to the stand."

Jennifer was sworn in and Petrie started questioning her, "what happened after you married."

"I ask to sleep in my room. Joe got angry and kept Little Fox outside my room. I couldn't go anywhere but in the house."

"And, did you ever get out of the house?"

"Yes. During a roundup. Everybody was drunk. I escaped."

"Why did you return to the ranch?" Petrie questioned.

"I called Joe to ask for a divorce," she answered, trying to pull her drifting thoughts together. She didn't want to mention Steven. "He came after me, threatened me and went back to the hotel where he stayed."

"Tell the court what happened next," Petrie said.

"Joe played cards with some men in his hotel room. Words were exchanged and he was shot in both knees."

"He had a fiery temper, did he not?"

"Yes," she said, at the point of tears.

"Your witness," Petrie nodded to the prosecutor.

Prosecutor Feldman stood directly in front of Jennifer. "You wanted your husband dead so you could be with your lover, didn't you?"

Petrie jumped to his feet. "Objections, your Honor. It hasn't been established that she has a lover."

"Objections sustained," Judge Black said, softly.

"What about the man you were seen with at the Hyatt Hotel?"

"I met him when I was in California," she said, her lips trembling. "We became friends."

"Come on now, Ms. Morgan, Didn't he ask you to marry him?"

Her thoughts filtered back to the day she'd met Steven, and how she'd grown to love everything about him: his warm smile, his easygoing manner and his thoughtfulness. She recalled the ecstasy of being held against his strong body, and the ache of desire at the thought of him now wracked her body with longing, and she answered, "He asked me after we'd known each other for a few short months.

His questions hammered at her. "Weren't you going to marry him? Didn't you want your husband out of the way?"

"I didn't want him dead," she said, with a long exhausted sigh. "I wanted a divorce to get on with my life."

Prosecutor Feldman faced the jury. "Yes. We all know why. And where is this lover now?"

"Objections! Petrie yelled. "Now the prosecutor is speculating, Your Honor."

"Objections sustained. I'm warning you, Mr. Prosecutor."

"We haven't been able to find this man for questioning, Your Honor. I'm through for now with Ms. Morgan. I call Mr. Morley again to the stand."

Morley took a seat on the stand and Prosecutor Feldman stood in front of him looking him in the eye. "Have you ever seen Ms. Morgan with another man?"

"Yes, Mr. Joe told me to follow her into town. She met a man at the Marriott Hotel."

"Did you ever see then kissing?"

"Yes, sir."

"No further question," Prosecutor Feldman said.

Mr. Petrie, do you wish to question this witness?"Judge Black asked.

"Yes, Your Honor. Mr. Morley, you said you saw them kissing. Were they embracing?"

"No, sir, he put his head inside the car and kissed her when she was leaving."

"Oh, he was saying goodbye!" exclaimed Mr. Petrie, facing the jury. "Kissing someone goodbye doesn't make them lovers." Mr. Petrie faced Morley. "Did she ever spend a night away from home?"

"No, sir, she always returned home."

"Thank you, Mr. Morley."

"You may step down, Mr. Morley," Judge Black said. "We'll recess and return at nine o'clock tomorrow morning for summation."

Jennifer went back to the ranch and stayed in her room. Her whole body was engulfed in tides of weariness and despair. Hollow and lifeless, she lay in bed. This was going to be a long night, and tomorrow, even longer and uncertain. Suppose she was found guilty? She couldn't stand being locked away, never to see Steven, or her family again. There had to be something in Joe's room that could reveal how he died. Detective Taylor and the police searched every inch of his room…yet, how did Joe know about her gun, and how did he reach the closet. He'd have to stand to remove it from the shelf, where she'd hidden it, after Bobby Ray left her room.

She hopped out of bed, and hurried to Joe's room, avoiding the bloodstained spot on the carpet where he had sat. She shuttered at the scent of his tobacco and whiskey, as she removed his pillow and pushed the head of the mattress forward. "What's this?" she murmured and lifted the black cord. "That sound…something in the wall vent."

She got a chair, stood on top, and removed the wall vent's cover. "A video camera? Ofcourse. She removed the camera, scurried to the den, and placed the video in the VCR. "Oh, my God!"

Bill heard her and ran to the room, confused and slightly thrown in reaction to her yelling. "What's happened?"

"I can prove my innocence. Look!"

Bill's eyes widened. "It's him. He's the shooter."

A chill ran down Jennifer's spine. "I've been frightened

throughout this trial. The prosecutor is hellbent on sending me to prison."

"Me, too. That Feldman is nuts."

"I've got to thank Bobby Ray."

"He's on leave. His mom broke her hip."

"I got to call Petrie." She dialed his number. "What's taking him so long? Oh, his answering machine." She left a message.

"This is your miracle," Bill said. "I don't know what you've done without this."

She squeezed his shoulder. "You're right. I'm not sure Petrie convinced the jury of my innocence." Her words settled in her brain. She shook her head and took a deep breath. "The judge won't take kindly to this short development."

"He seems fair. It's Feldman who'll protest."

She waited till midnight for Petrie's call. When he didn't, she put the video in a brown paper bag on the desk.

"Get some sleep, Sis. You have a promising day tomorrow."

The early morning sun shown brightly through Jennifer's window, as she turned over and yawned. It was peaceful and serene, quiet but not too quiet. The ranch hands were herding horses into the carrel. She got up and peered through the curtains, as Bill mounted one of the horses. *He's learned well for a city boy, and fitted into this life more than she had.*

She showered, dressed and went to the den for the video. "For the love of God! She knelt down, supporting herself with one hand on the desk and the other searching under the desk. Then, she screamed for the maid, "There was a bag on this desk."

"Sorry, Mistress, I thought it to be trash."

"Nooo." Her hands formed into fists. She wanted to curse out loud, but she gritted her teeth and yelled, "Do you realize what you've done?"

She ran outside to Bill. "I'm dead."

"What?"

"The video was thrown in the trash, and the trash man's come and gone."

Bill jumped off his horse. "Don't worry. Go to court. I'll find it."

"How? Oh, dear God, there won't be time!"

"I'll track him down. He's gotta be in the neighborhood."

Anxiety gripped her as she got in her car and drove to town.

Petrie greeted her with a smile when she sat at the table. "I got your message this morning…late night. Let's have the video."

"I don't have it," she said her head bowed.

Petrie almost fell out of his chair.

"It was thrown in the trash."

"You're kidding, right?"

"No."

Petrie looked at her with his mouth agape.

She would bet he wondered how in the world she could let something happen to the video. "I can't believe it either."

She was about to give him the details when the clerk entered.

"All rise."

"Be seated," Judge Black commanded. "Mr. Petrie are you ready for your summation?"

"Yes, Your Honor. Ladies and gentlemen of the jury. The prosecutor has not proved his case. The defendant did all she could for a man who tricked her into marriage and held her against her will. When she asked him for a divorce, he again tricked her. When she wanted to leave him, he tried to kill her, but ended up dying himself. All she ever did was to help him. Now, I ask you, ladies and gentlemen, does that sound like a woman who would commit murder? Send this woman home, and let her get on with her life."

"Ladies and gentlemen, Mr. Petrie would have you believe that Ms. Morgan was a dutiful wife, caring for her invalid husband, the one she wanted to leave," Prosecutor Feldman said. "He would have you believe that she came back to help a man she said tricked her into marriage." Mr. Feldman went down the row appealing to each juror. "Ms. Morgan wanted to have her cake and eat it too. She wanted her lover and what her husband had to offer. She seized the moment, when they argued, to do what she waited for; kill him and claim self-defense. I say she's a cold-blooded murderer. I think you ladies and gentlemen will agree and find her guilty of murder in the first degree."

"The jury will retire and we'll recess till two o'clock," Judge Black said.

Jennifer stumbled out of the court and Petrie took her arm. "You look pale. Did you eat anything this morning?"

"Food wasn't on my mind. Had I eaten, I wouldn't have kept it in my stomach. My stomach is in nervous knots."

"Come on, let's get some lunch," Petrie suggested. "My treat. We'll go to Roger's Restaurant."

Jennifer and Petrie were seated and given a menu. "I'll have the fried chicken," Jennifer said.

"Give me the pot roast and iced tea," Petrie said, looking around. "What's he doing here?"

Jennifer turned and looked at a tall man, dressed in a western outfit, with a wide straw hat, long dark hair, thick mustache, beard, and bushy eyebrows. "There's something familiar about his eyes."

"He's sat in the court room, behind us in the front row, since the trial began," Petrie noted.

"Why is he following us? What does he want?" Jennifer asked, glancing at him.

"I'll go find out. If he gets smart, I'll punch him out."

"No. Let's eat our food and go. I don't want any more trouble." Jennifer finished her food and thought of Steven. His name lingered around the edges of her mind.

Petrie glanced at his watch. "Ready to go? It's one o'clock."

She sighed, shrugged, and got up to leave. "Let's get it over with."

Inside the court room, the jury had returned. "Ladies and gentlemen, have you reached a verdict?"

"We have, Your Honor."

"Hand it to the clerk." Judge Black looked at the verdict and was about to hand it back to the clerk, when Bill rushed inside and handed Jennifer the video.

Judge Black banged his gavel. "What is this disturbance? Who is he?"

"Your Honor, I got new evidence to prove my client's innocence," Petrie said.

The court room buzzed. Everyone looked puzzled.

Judge black banged his gavel. "Quiet!"

Prosecutor Feldman jumped to his feet. "Say, what is he trying to pull? Why didn't he come forward sooner? It's too late."

"I'll decide when it's too late," Judge Black said. "I want to see all of you in my chamber right now!"

They followed Judge Black and stood in front of his desk. "What is this new evidence?

Why didn't you come forward with it sooner?"

"It was lost, Your Honor," Bill said. "I found it this morning."

"Ok, lets see the tape," Judge Black said, taking it and inserting it into his VCR.

"You can see," Jennifer said. "I ran out of the room."

Bill pointed to the picture. "There's Lil' Fox."

"Judge Black shushed him, "Let's hear what they're saying."

"Take the gun and shoot me," Joe commanded. "You owe me your life."

Little Fox backed away with a look of horror on his face. "No. You're like a father to me."

"I can't live alone and crippled," Joe cried. "Shoot me!"

Feldman's eyes widened with amazement, and he stared with his mouth agape.

"Wait! Not your gun," Little Fox said. He left out and returned with Jennifer's gun. He hugged joe, held the gun to his head, and fired.

Judge Black, placed a call to his clerk. "Send an officer to the Morgan ranch and bring Little Fox in for murder."

"Congratulations, Petrie," Feldman said and shook his hand. "And, I misjudged you, Ms. Morgan."

"Yes, you did, sir, and I'm happy you were proven wrong."

They returned to the court room and Judge Black banged his gavel and made an announcement, "Ladies and gentlemen of the jury, new evidence now renders the defendant innocent of all charges. He looked at Jennifer and said, "You are free to leave, Ms. Morgan." Then said to the jury, "Ladies and gentlemen, thank you for your time. You are here by dismissed."

The man seated in the first row, behind Jennifer, jumped across the seats, peeled his beard, mustache and eyebrows, and threw his wig in the air. He grabbed her and held her in his arms.

"Steven! You've been here all along," she said, and kissed him. "And, you followed us."

"Of course, I'd never leave you alone."

They left out of the court room surrounded by dozens of reporters. Steven rushed Jennifer out to his car and sped away.

Petrie wanted to know what the jury had decided about Jennifer and he cornered Judge Black. "What was the verdict?"

Judge Black handed him the slip of paper. Petrie's eyes grew wide, and he blew hard. "It's a good thing Bobby Ray made that video."

"Justice is served," Judge Black noted. "Let's go home."

Two days later, Jennifer held Joe's funeral at the ranch. He would lay buried on a grassy hill overlooking the stables of his favorite horses.

Little Fox hid himself from the police until the day of the funeral. Officers waited there, in case he'd show. As the funeral director lowered the casket into the ground, Little fox rushed out from behind the oak tree, shading Joe's burial spot, wailed, slit his throat and fell upon Joe's coffin.

Everyone screamed and covered their eyes and mouth in horror. Jennifer fainted in Steven's arms.

The burial was delayed for an hour, until everyone got control of their nerves, and to let the coroners recover Little Fox's body.

Several days later, Jennifer buried Little Fox next to Joe, and the next day, she and Steven flew to Los Angeles. Gracie and Tanya celebrated that night.

"Your wedding and reception are going to be held here," Gracie said, with her arms around them.

Tanya nudged Gracie and slid between them. "Please, may I be your maiden of honor?"

"I want all my family present," Jennifer said, beaming. "Mama and Mr. Jack are coming next week. And, Jack may come in his wheelchair."

"Good God!" Tanya exclaimed. "He sat in his wheelchair? It must've taken a lot for Mamma to get him out a' bed." She laughed and threw her hands in the air. "Lord. There's hope for us all."

The End

Printed in the United States
47929LVS00002B/1-15

9 781413 758603